ETHER

THE WANDERING PROSPECTOR'S FORTUNE

RENEE YUKSEL

All quotations from scripture are taken from the King James Version of the Bible.

This book is a work of fiction. Although it is based on real events, the author has created characters, names, and places through their imagination or used them fictitiously.

Cover Design: by Stefan P.

Published by Strolling Donkeys, LLC, 30 N Gould St STE N, Sheridan, WY 82801

WWW.strollingdonkeys.com

Our mission is to help readers understand the importance of a personal relationship with Jesus Christ.

ISBN-13 979-8-9989104-6-3

❀ Formatted with Vellum

To Jesus Chris for always showing up when no one else would.

CHAPTER 1

*C*hicago, IL 2288

I multitask between deep thought and taking in the view outside my window during the tour. I came along because I enjoy history, but I find this chapter particularly depressing, given the extent of the destruction that once occurred. Yet the resilience of nature persists and regenerates, allowing the earth to heal and create new life while preserving evidence of vast devastation, all within the same landscape.

I'm lucky to have a window seat, and even being on a tour bus feels historical in its own way. I focus on the surroundings as I smile and interact with those around me. I had nothing planned for this weekend, so getting out, meeting new people, and sightseeing would be a fun way to spend my time.

At times, the road can be distracting, especially when we hit potholes. The streets haven't been paved in a long time and likely won't be again, since modern society no longer needs them. I admit it's a bit depressing to think about what once was and what could have been. As I gaze out the window, the tour bus moves slowly, but my thoughts drift to work. I can't figure something out, and it's driving me crazy.

I remember the stories my grandmother used to tell me about the past and how, to visit the ruins, she had to wear a gas mask. Now that radiation levels have returned to normal, such measures are no longer necessary. I've never told anyone, but I find the dilapidated buildings overgrown by nature strangely beautiful.

You can even tell the time of day it happened by what's left behind. The bus drives past rusted bicycles in front of crumbling, small dwellings that were once homes. It happened during the afternoon—just another day for many.

As the bus shakes and bumps along, I begin to form a plan to resolve my work issue. I feel more confident about solving it as I reflect on my options. I think I'll ask the Professor about it. Just then, the bus hits a massive pothole, causing me to bounce out of my seat. I realize we're getting very close to the epicenter—ground zero for Chicago in 2180. Now, I can see the skeletal remains of skyscrapers that once symbolized success and life, now serving as reminders of what a prosperous society shouldn't become, or what it shouldn't do in pursuit of life.

The nuclear bombs were designed for both ground targets, leaving craters, and airbursts that caused nuclear winter across much of the world during World War III. Several cities in the United States were affected, particularly Chicago, New York, and Los Angeles. Even though it happened a hundred years ago, life was permanently altered. At least in America, survivors blamed and denounced the government, forming city-states instead. Several of these were established, and since the ground and air were contaminated, large, massive dome structures were built for each city-state.

These buildings are enormous and elevated, supported by massive cement columns that extend several stories above ground, allowing animals and plants to roam freely beneath them. The dome structures have half-cement bases and half-glass tops, creating a second atmosphere for the city. The air was once regulated and protected from radiation or another potential nuclear attack. Now that radiation levels have returned to normal at ground-zero sites, evacuation may no longer be necessary. However, people remain reluctant to return to their old way of life. These structures offer much greater safety and security in case a nuclear war ever happens again.

The siding on the domes combines solar panels and mirrors, which generate energy and reflect light, supporting the growth of plants and wildlife beneath. The lowest level of the dome structure is about five stories high, providing ample space for trees and birds to thrive.

Everything changed after World War III, primarily how society functions. Now, people view their city-state as their country and focus locally on surviving in tight-knit communities. Glass-covered subway trains connect the city-states, running on magnets to propel them at relatively high speeds.

There are stations where people can take elevators or walk up and down staircases to return to the ground surface. It's been a while since I've been down here. It's not always safe. Not everyone joined a city-state—some stayed on the ground, away from the ground-zero locations, and formed their own groups. They're called rebels, as they can sometimes be aggressive in their pursuit of resources and violent in their attempts to acquire them.

Not everyone in the world had the resources to build such structures so quickly. We didn't either, at first. Some people survived the nuclear bombs but suffered DNA changes from the radiation, and their mutated offspring became known as "the others." It's not a term often used in polite society, but nonetheless, it refers to another group that exists outside the city-states. They have their own towns and communities. We don't mingle with them, just as we don't with the rebels. It might not end well if we did, as competition for resources also exists with the others.

The lady beside me tries to make conversation about the tour and shares her thoughts on seeing the abandoned city of Chicago. She says it's hard to believe it used to be one of the largest cities in America. I have to agree as I look out at the building rubble and skeletal remains of structures overgrown with plants—even trees—scattered everywhere.

A beeping sound comes from the tour bus driver's alarm on her belt clip. That usually means one of two things: either rebels are nearby or the others are. The tour guide announces that we'll head back toward the station. Rebels or others typically won't attack a station, since advanced defenses are in place, but they might target a small group of people out like we are now. The bus has defenses, but it's better to be safe than sorry.

After driving for a while, the alarm goes off again, prompting the driver to make a gradual U-turn. She informs us that we won't go as far into the downtown center but will stop shortly to let us look around. Eventually, the bus stops, and we get out. The air has a stale, heavy scent mixed with an oddly strong floral aroma. You'd expect the air to be fresh, but it's not. I start walking and looking around. Rusted cars and trucks surround crumbling buildings that once appeared to be gray office buildings, situated near a large parking lot. In the distance, I see some tall buildings, though not skyscrapers. Some members of the tour group want to go inside, but the guide tells us it's unsafe.

She informs the group that the buildings have been left unattended for a long time and are in a state of disrepair. I walk around, watching everyone in the group snapping pictures and milling about. I begin to feel lonely as I see people enjoying each other's company. I moved to a different city-state a while back for a job opportunity, and ever since, I haven't made many friends. I work a lot and didn't know anyone from the city-state of Sanctuary.

I walk toward a building shell that catches my eye because of the plants growing there—dogwood trees, stiff goldenrod, milkweed, and New England aster. The building is a single-story structure with no doors and broken windows. People have thrown rocks through them. There's no roof either. The tour guide explains that the rebels and others have stripped some of the building materials over the years. It's not all just natural decay.

As I look around the building, I begin to feel like I'm being watched. The feeling only grows stronger the more I try to ignore it. I turn and scan the area to see if anyone is there. I notice the parking lot, its asphalt cracked and broken, with weeds and grass growing between the rusted cars. Something about it doesn't feel right. Someone is watching me.

I turn again and see a figure in the distance. Unease creeps in as the figure moves out of view behind thick foliage and more buildings. I immediately glance at the tour bus driver to see if her alarm has gone off, but it hasn't. That strikes me as odd. Something about this feels wrong.

I start heading toward the bus when I hear a faint voice calling my name. I turn around and see the dark, blurred figure again, standing and staring at me. I freeze, unsure of what to do. The figure remains, unmoving. I glance around, scanning the area. Off in the distance to my left, I see the tour group. My focus shifts back to the figure as my peripheral vision clears, and the unsettling sense of being watched returns.

The figure walks a bit closer, and I see that it appears to be male based on his clothing. He seems to be dressed in dark-colored cowboy attire, complete with a black cowboy hat. I feel uneasy as he takes a few more steps forward and calls my name again.

He stands there and, in a deep and commanding tone, calls out to me one last time, "Desiree."

I begin to walk backward, trying to put more distance between us. As he comes a bit closer, I can see more clearly that he is another—his light grey skin, tall, thin frame, and iridescent light magenta eyes give him away. He's strikingly handsome, both in face and figure, even from a distance, but there's something otherworldly about him. Though still human, his DNA has clearly been mutated by the radiation.

With a shaky voice, I ask if I know him. He replies, "No, but you will soon enough." I'm unsure what to make of this, and I start to feel either threatened or like it's an omen. I'm not sure which, so I decide to head back to the tour bus, still walking in reverse and watching him closely.

He stands there for a moment, watching me watch him, then turns around and walks away. I stop and watch as he disappears into the foliage and crumbling buildings. Then suddenly, a blue-colored light flashes from the ground up. The same stale air I noticed when I first arrived hits my nose again.

I immediately glance at the tour group, who are still enjoying their sightseeing, seemingly unaware of anything unusual. I keep staring at the place where I saw the figure, but he's completely gone. I'm baffled, sure that something strange just happened—and that I was the only one who saw it.

I walk back to the bus, get on, and return to my seat, still thinking about what just occurred. Eventually, more passengers return to their seats, and we depart. I begin to feel that I should have followed when I saw the blue light, to see if anything was there. It might have been a clue to what the strange man meant when he said I would know him soon enough.

The bus heads out, and we're on our way back to the city, which is called Sanctuary. I feel distraught, as no one else around me seems to notice anything unusual. The lady next to me started talking about what she saw and how interesting it all was to her. I nod in agreement, though my thoughts remain fixed on the strange encounter.

We arrive back at the station, get off the bus, and head to the elevators.

They're protected by a nearly invisible force field that can be activated in the event of a threat. The elevators are impressive, with strong steel doors. There are eight large ones, and when I step inside, I notice each features a floor-to-ceiling window at the back. I stand near the window and look out as we ascend. Below, I see a grassy field scattered with oak trees and birds flying through the air.

When we reach the top, the elevator opens onto a large deck with clear glass balcony railings. Stone benches are placed in the middle of the deck, as natural materials are prioritized over man-made ones. I sit on one of the benches and wait for a train to arrive. After about fifteen minutes, one pulls in, and I get on.

The trains are white and feature a sleek, aerodynamic design. The seats are arranged in vertical rows, similar to those on a standard train, and everyone picks an available seat.

Once the train departs, it speeds through a clear plastic tube. Because of the high speed and the tube itself, there's not much to see out the window. When we arrive, I step out onto a deck that leads into the city. Sanctuary is entirely walkable, though trams run long distances throughout. I head toward my apartment, which isn't too far. The city is built on terraces that gradually narrow as you ascend.

I stroll through the city, admiring the small shops that are beautifully designed with large bay windows, flower beds on the sills, and wide wooden doors with arched frames. Water fountains cascade down the terraces through stone slides, leading into basins that overflow and send water further down, continuing this cycle throughout the city. Large open-air patios are often arranged around these fountains, with tables and chairs set up for people to gather and converse. Canopies are strung between poles to shield visitors from the sun during the day, and porch-style white lights are turned on to illuminate the area at night. Potted and hanging flowers are everywhere, lining the city's beautifully crafted, winding stone walkways.

I make my way home by climbing staircases made of shatter-resistant colored glass. After ascending five flights, I turn left and pass four doors until I reach my apartment on the right. To the left is a stone railing made of the same colorful glass as the stairs. The thick glass allows partial views of the walkways below. Azaleas grow over the railing in front of the nearby apartments, and I enjoy seeing them—it always cheers me up.

I arrive at my front door, painted a light mint green. Residents paint their doors in a wide range of colors and decorate them with distinctive shapes and designs. Mine is made of heavy wood, with floral patterns etched into its surface. On either side of the door is a large window, each with a plant box on the sill where I grow wildflowers. Thanks to the glass dome above the city, we enjoy a regulated temperature year-round. It's kept at a constant 78 degrees, allowing us to grow plants in every season.

I have several potted plants around both windows. There's even a rocking chair painted the same color as my front door, with pink roses painted on the flat back spindles. It also features a pink cushion. I open the large brass doorknob and step inside. My ceiling is a mural of colored glass forming patterns, since I live in an apartment without a terrace above mine. I'm on the edge of my terrace in the city's center. From here, I can look down and see all the pavilions below, people walking around, and the colored glass walkways and ceilings of the lower terraces and decks.

My floor is made of tan stone, with a large multicolored area rug placed where my two tan wicker chairs and tan wicker couch sit. The sofa is positioned against the right wall, with the chairs facing it. The back wall features a balcony and French glass doors with sheer pink curtains.

Oscar greets me as I come in—my tabby cat. He rubs against my leg in greeting. Just to the right of the front door is the kitchen, and on the left side is a small dining area across from it.

To the left of the living room is a short hallway that leads to my bedroom and bathroom. Oscar has a bed to the right of the couch. He yawns, returns to the sofa, and curls up there to sleep again. I walk over to my desk, located behind the kitchen wall, and begin jotting down notes about everything I want to research tomorrow at work. I also take notes on the strange person I saw—or met—today, though I'm still not sure which it was.

CHAPTER 2

*T*he next day, I head off to work. I leave the house, turn right, open the door, and climb more stone steps. After going up a flight of stairs, I arrive at a pavilion featuring a cascading waterfall and several wrought-iron tables and chairs. No one is sitting at them this early in the morning. An iced tea would be lovely as I relax at one of the tables in passing, heading for the tram.

I take another right and walk past some shops that are just opening for the day. The stores are housed in smaller, boutique-style rooms, but there's a variety of establishments, including supermarkets and clothing stores.

I continue, passing several shops and outdoor vendors with booths set up to sell fresh produce. The lower terraces are reserved for agriculture, allowing for year-round food production. Each city-state has its own unique currency system. This particular city-state, known as Sanctuary, uses silver coins in various denominations, each engraved with images of former leaders. The founding father of Sanctuary is Raymond Taylor, and I hear a lot about him here. Eighty years ago, he provided most of the funds to a wealthy financier to build the city.

Up ahead are the trams. The tram station features automatic glass doors, and instrumental music plays over the intercom and air conditioning systems. The station sits along the inner terrace on a track that loops continuously. On the other side of the station are the backs of buildings made of various bricks and stones, decorated with stained-glass patterns.

I wait patiently for the white tram, joined by another man. After a while, the tram arrives, and I get on. I sit on a white seat with a gray cushion that matches the carpet along the white side panels of the tram. The center remains open to accommodate standing passengers, bicycles, and baby strollers. There's no jerking motion when the tram takes off, as it's powered by magnetic friction rather than a mechanical engine.

The trams move slowly within the city, so it will take some time to reach my destination. I look out the tram windows on the opposite side and take in the open view of the city. It resembles a cascading series of buildings inside a circular dome, with colorful glass ceilings along the outer terrace edges, canopies in pavilions, and lush plants and flowers throughout. The city is massive, with a population of over 300,000.

I arrive at my stop as the tram pulls into the station. I get off while the man in the back stays on. I head straight toward the station exit and follow the path outside. Turning left, I continue walking past a mix of homes and shops. Ahead on the left is my workplace—the Museum of Modern History and Science.

The building is a large, cream-colored stone structure. I open the heavy doors and enter a long hallway. I walk straight past the ticket window and the lobby, then go through a cream-colored door marked "Employees Only." At the back wall is an elevator, and I press the button to go up. To the left are lockers and a sitting area.

There's no window at the back of the elevator, just a mirror. I press the button for the third floor, and once the elevator reaches it, the doors open. I step into a hallway and walk down to the fourth door on the right. This is where the museum stores artifacts from the previous excavation at Cemetery Hill.

I'M an archaeologist employed by the museum, originally hired as a curator for the collections. Recently, I was transferred to the lab to analyze artifacts, soil samples, flora, and fauna found at the excavation site in Arizona at Cemetery Hill. The site was once a bustling Old West boomtown, known for a legendary shootout that has inspired many books and films.

The project is funded by the university here in Sanctuary. The university offers a summer field school for archaeologists to learn field techniques and methods. Oddly, the university asked the museum to handle the lab work rather than doing it themselves, especially since this would be a valuable opportunity for students to gain experience. The museum director is good friends with the university's archaeology professor, and I sense that this connection significantly influences why our lab is processing the excavation findings instead of the university's. But I still wonder why.

Suddenly, the door opens, and in walks Professor Wendell Murphy. He's a short, stout, overweight middle-aged man with a bald spot and hair that's whitening. He has a professional demeanor, but I sense a certain coldness underneath.

He greets me without a smile and asks about my progress, his blue eyes fixed on me. I give him all the details, and he seems a little indecisive about it. He reminds me that he wants everything finished soon so it can be shipped back to a museum in Arizona. Again, it's strange that the Arizona museum wasn't tasked with processing the findings themselves, especially since I'm handling it here in Illinois. The whole situation feels odd.

Prior to the federal government's establishment, land had to be surveyed for archaeology before it could be built on or modified. Private cultural resource firms handled the surveys and lab work and returned everything to the property owner. Universities often conducted surveys or excavations, including field schools, when invited by landowners or institutions to give students hands-on experience.

Wendell leaves, and I return to my computer. I call out the name "Octavius." A low "hello" answers from my desk. I walk over to see a holographic man with dark hair, dressed in a tuxedo, about a foot tall. I ask Octavius about specific lab tests performed on soil samples, and a beam of light projects from the hologram, creating a screen of light that displays the results in an Excel-style spreadsheet.

I review the data and instruct Octavius to log the results into the report. He pauses as a digital chime sounds. I walk over and open a new box of artifacts to process. Inside are several clear bags labeled with the site name and contents. I take a deep breath before beginning, and suddenly, Octavius starts singing "Puttin' on the Ritz" as he dances around in his tuxedo.

I laugh and dance a little in place, then notice something on the table—Wendell must have left it behind by accident. It's a type of electronic device featuring a large blue stone at its center. I place it in the upper right drawer of my desk and lock it for safekeeping until I can return it to him.

I tell Octavius we're heading home to see Oscar. He looks up at me from where he stands on the desk and starts dancing around with joy. I pick him up and place him on my shoulder as I head out of the lab. The room has white walls and cabinets lined along them, with various testing equipment set on the cabinet counters. White tables fill the center of the room, where artifacts, soil samples, and other materials are processed and logged into the database. Along the left wall, near the entrance, shipping boxes are stacked in areas where cabinets are absent.

I tell Octavius we can finish processing tomorrow. As I leave the lab, I realize he's always been with me for as long as I can remember. In this era, everyone is assigned a personal holographic teacher from an early age—customized to each student—teaching everything from reading and writing in grade school to organic chemistry in college.

I keep Octavius on my shoulder as I head home by tram. I've known for a while that he's my closest friend. I watch people passing by with families or groups of friends heading off together. I often wonder why I don't have that in my life. Octavius has always been a cheerful bundle of positivity. I wish I could be like that, but I've always leaned toward pessimism.

When we get home, Octavius lets Oscar chase him all around the house. Sometimes, Octavius even rides on Oscar's back. I watch them run around, having fun together. I sit on the couch with an iced tea and a mystery novel for the evening. At bedtime, Oscar curls up next to me, while Octavius returns to his charging station on my desk in the living room—a round, white disk that resembles a drink coaster. In charging mode, Octavius appears to be sleeping in a small bed with an oak headboard and footboard, wearing blue and white striped pajamas and a matching nightcap. The comforter is a multicolored quilt.

The next day at work, I'm in the supply room looking for various items when I hear someone enter, only for them to suddenly stop and leave the

11

door slightly ajar. I recognize Wendell's voice talking to the museum director, Ms. Collins. They appear to be arguing. Wendell promises her he'll find the Ether device he lost yesterday. Ms. Collins tells him he'd better—because if Damien handles it, they both know what that would mean. She adds that it'll be bad enough for all of us if he takes over the world with the Ether device.

Then Wendell says he might have left it in Louis's office, or possibly in Desiree's lab. Ms. Collins interjects, "Then we'll just have to kill her to get it back," chuckling with a serious tone. "I never really liked her anyway," she adds. Wendell insists they need to check both offices. Then the door suddenly shuts, and I hear their footsteps fading down the hallway.

I wait a minute or two before quietly leaving the supply closet. Peeking into the hallway, I make sure no one is around. It's empty. I hurry to my office to grab the Ether device and Octavius. At my desk, I unlock the drawer using my electronic thumbprint and retrieve a slim, dark gray device. I place it in my purse. It features a blue oval crystal in the upper center and displays two sets of electronic digital coordinates.

I pick up Octavius, who is looking at me rather oddly, as I make my way out of the lab. I keep glancing from side to side as I head out of the building and toward the trams. I walk briskly—fast enough to hurry but not so fast as to draw too much attention. I'm thinking about where I can go to get away for a while. I know it will be evident that I took the Ether device, but I'm not thinking rationally right now.

I'm considering visiting one of the Orbit farms. In the city-states, we grow food in glass spheres kept near Earth's orbit. The food is cultivated using terrace agriculture, with one vast slope facing the sun. There are about fifteen of these orbit farms, and it's usually easy to get a ticket to visit one. Some nearby hotels cater to families who occasionally bring their children, since the farms also feature a space-themed attraction.

Then I think about going back to my birth city-state and staying with my family. I haven't seen them in years, and it would be nice to have company for a change. So many ideas are running through my mind right now. All I really want is to get home, pack, and grab Oscar. I don't believe I'll be coming back for a while.

I arrive at the tram station near my workplace and stand waiting for the next one, gazing up at the multicolored glass roof and the matching walk-way. I have an odd feeling that all of this will someday become a distant memory. A tram arrives, and I board while scanning the area for either Wendell or Ms. Collins. I keep focusing, looking for Ms. Collins—a tall, thin woman with light blonde hair in a bob and dark blue eyes. She always wears a white lab coat, though I never figured out why, since she doesn't work in the lab. I begin to breathe a little slower and feel less anxious, as it doesn't seem like anyone is following me.

I walk home feeling a bit more at ease, though Octavius keeps his eyes on me most of the way. He seems concerned and clearly senses something is very wrong. When I arrive, I head straight to the bedroom and throw some clothes and toiletries into a suitcase. Then I move to the living room, grab Octavius's charging pad, and suddenly hear a noise coming from the kitchen. I realize I'm not alone.

I spot Oscar in the hallway, scoop him up, and hold him under my right arm. Octavius is still perched on my shoulder as I hear footsteps approach-ing. I look toward the kitchen and see Wendell and Ms. Collins standing there with smug grins.

Ms. Collins says she suspected I took the Ether device. Wendell steps forward with what looks like a Taser in his hand. I know I need to get out, but I'm trapped—my only options are the hallway or the back of the living room. Instinctively, I choose the hallway. I figure I can lock the bedroom door and buy a little time to think. I grab the suitcase, tell Octavius to hang on tight, clutch Oscar under my arm, and bolt for the bedroom. As I'm running, I hear what sounds like two gunshots just as I reach the door.

I get inside and immediately slam it shut, locking it behind me. A few seconds later, the knob begins to rattle wildly as I hear Wendell and Ms. Collins yelling at each other about how to break in. Then the door itself starts to shake violently, cracking at the right side of the frame as Wendell kicks it.

I turn to look around the room for options. My eyes land on the Ether device. I grab it and stare, wondering what all the fuss is about. I press the center of the device, and it lights up with a blue glow, displaying digital remote controls in a central console format.

I press "Enter"—it seems like the simplest option—and the coordinates at the top turn green. Then I feel the device start to vibrate, expanding quickly. Suddenly, a blue, pulsating beam shoots out from the top of the device, which I happen to be pointing at the back wall of the bedroom. The beam creates a glowing blue circle on the wall, resembling a portal.

I can now see the portal forming clearly, and it looks as if I could walk right through it into what appears to be an old pioneer house in the desert. Just then, my attention snaps back to the door as I hear it give way—Wendell and Ms. Collins barge into my bedroom. Ms. Collins rushes toward me and the device, but I grab my luggage and Oscar, with Octavius screaming as he clings to my shoulder, and I leap through the portal.

Immediately, I feel the force of the vibrational energy; it's thick and heavy as I move through it. It pulsates through me, and I become very still, unaware of Wendell, Ms. Collins, or even the lab coat. Suddenly, there's a flash of blinding white light, and I feel the energy around me stop. I'm more or less dumped out of the portal into standard time and space, surrounded by the same strong, stale air.

I turn back just in time to see the portal close behind me. I wasn't followed. I wonder if they couldn't come through or if they chose not to, even though they were just inches away.

I look ahead in disbelief, trying to fathom where I am—and how I'm going to get back home as soon as possible.

CHAPTER 3

I realize I've collapsed and find myself sitting on the ground as I come back to full consciousness. I can feel the sun on me and begin to sweat a little at my brow. Looking ahead, I see a woman staring directly at me. After a moment of staring back, I catch a glimpse of a young man also watching me. I decide to get up and dust off my clothes. Taking a panoramic glance at my surroundings, I realize I'm in a desert and, from the looks of things, nowhere near the 2280s.

Ahead, I see a large, weathered wooden Victorian house that looks old and in need of some repair. Still, it's kept clean and cheerful, with window boxes of flowers and white rocking chairs on the front porch.

I can tell the young man keeps his gaze on me, even when I look away and glance back. He's dressed in a tan-striped long-sleeve shirt, suspenders, and brown pants. He wears brown leather boots and a brown gambler's hat. He's slim, with brown hair, dark eyes, and an olive complexion. His appearance is plain, but there's something quietly handsome about him.

The woman in front of me has flaming red hair styled in side braids. She has dark blue eyes, a very fair complexion, and freckles across her face. She wears a wide-brimmed straw hat to block the sun, a blue and cream checkered apron, and a simple blue long-sleeve dress with dark brown leather boots.

I begin walking toward the dirt road on the right when I hear the woman say, "You need a change of clothes to fit in around here. I don't know where you came from, but I know you wound up in the right place."

She introduces herself. "My name is Victoria, but everyone calls me Vicki for short. The fella over there is Ollie. Welcome to Rocky Creek."

Ollie waves, still staring at me. I feel a little awkward standing there. Vicki motions for me to come over as she introduces her home. She tells me it's considered the town orphanage and a place for those in need. She also mentions that three widows live on the property.

I scan the yard of the house and see a large cotton field with a smaller cornfield. Vicki notices me looking at the fields and tells me there's an orchard in the back with grapevines and date trees. She also says they grow potatoes, along with various herbs and vegetables, since they have a well and access to the town's river, which isn't too far away.

Vicki explains that the corn is used to feed the hogs, which are sold to support the orphanage. Cotton is cultivated to make clothing and household items like tablecloths and bedding. Everything is made to order—if someone requests a lavender tablecloth of a specific size, she dyes the cotton and makes it herself.

I look at Vicki, impressed by how business-minded she seems. She adds that some of the grapes are used to make jams, and some of the dates are picked and sold.

I tell her she has a good setup to support the orphanage. She looks at me and explains that the home was donated by a wealthy family who moved on to better opportunities. Other than that, no one else offers help or financial support. The orphanage's survival depends on finding ways to sustain itself, or it will have to close.

She explains that it's more than just an orphanage, as she also helps others in need.

I don't know Vicki, but from what I can see, I think she's a good person. I begin to wonder why Ollie is here and glance over at him. He's walked back to where I was originally standing. He bends down and picks something up from the ground. It's the Ether device, along with my luggage. I'd completely forgotten about it in my shock.

I hear a cat meowing and look to the left side of the house. Oscar and

Octavius are hiding in a shrub. Oscar's meowing catches the attention of both Vicki and Ollie. Vicki turns to me and asks if I have a cat, and I tell her I do. She informs me that the cat will have to stay outside because of the flies. I reassure her that Oscar gets flea treatment every month. Vicki looks at me, puzzled, and asks what I mean by flea treatment every month. That's when I begin to realize—I've gone back to the past.

Ollie walks over to the shrub, and I start to feel nervous—what if he sees Octavius? Just then, an orange cat with a black bow tie emerges, and I know it's Octavius, updating his appearance. Ollie smiles and says he's made a friend as Octavius steps out of the bush.

Oscar and Octavius follow me, and Vicki watches them in horror as they approach the house. Oscar climbs onto the front porch and stops to sniff the rocking chairs. Vicki quickly slips inside, and I close the door behind us. I glance around the living room. It's simple, with wooden furniture that seems smaller than what I'm used to. An upright piano sits against the back wall.

The home is well-furnished, with long, ornate purple velvet curtains. Vicki notices me looking around and explains that everything came with the house. The wealthy family that donated it left all the furnishings behind when they bought new ones for their new home. Over time, she says, the place has started to feel a bit old-fashioned. I think to myself, *You have no idea how old-fashioned everything here feels to me.*

Vicki leads me to a small room off the kitchen and tells me it used to be the maid's quarters. Now, it serves as the orphanage's guest bedroom. Smiling, she says I'm a guest and need a place to stay for the night.

"If you need to stay longer," she adds, "you can help out with the household chores."

I feel a wave of relief—at least I have a place to stay while I figure out how to get back home. Vicki leaves, then returns with an olive green dress, similar to hers, and a pair of black leather boots. She hands them to me and says they belonged to her sister, Raquel. I hesitate and tell her I can't accept the dress, but she sighs and says Raquel may not be able to return for her things. I can sense something more personal beneath her words.

Just then, we hear Ollie come in. He sets the Ether device on the dining room table before heading out again. Vicki suddenly calls out, asking if he'd like to stay for dinner. Ollie smiles at me and politely declines, saying he'll take her up on the offer at the end of the week when he returns for his order.

"Alright," Vicki says, waving goodbye.

Ollie waves at me, and I wave back as I say goodbye.

After Ollie leaves, Vicki explains that he's one of her better customers, buying what he can from the orphanage to support it. I ask what he does for a living to be considered one of her best. Vicki tells me his family owns a cattle ranch. I think to myself, That's interesting—I've traveled back in time and met an actual cowboy.

Just then, two women enter the kitchen through a side door in the back wall. Each is carrying a basket of vegetables and dates from the garden. One has curly blonde ringlets and smiles at me. She doesn't look much older than I am, and I assume she's one of the widows living here.

Vicki introduces us. "This is Priscilla—uh, I don't think I got your name yet?"

"My name is Desiree," I say, and both women look puzzled by the situation—a guest Vicki hasn't even named.

"It's nice to meet you, Desiree," exclaims Priscilla.

She glances at the other woman and adds, "Oh, this is Matilda."

I smile at Matilda, but she doesn't return it. She sets her basket down on a stand and says she's going to serve the beef stew from the pot on the wood-burning stove. I could have sworn I saw her pick up a contact case from the stand and slip it into her pocket. She ladles the stew into a lovely china dish for the dining table. I feel a bit awkward. When she's done, she carries the dish into the dining room, with Priscilla following close behind. As they leave, I hear Priscilla ask if she knows who I am. Matilda replies that she has no idea, but everyone knows Vicki is constantly taking in strays.

Her comment stings. It feels like a dismissal of who I am. I don't know if Vicki heard it, but if she did, she chose to ignore it. Still, she's been kind to take me in for the night, and maybe I'll see Ollie again. I decide not to let it get me down.

. . .

18

I FOLLOW Vicki into the dining room, where seven children are already seated, along with Matilda and Priscilla. The dining table is long and rectangular, with twelve chairs. It's quite beautiful, made of mahogany. Two seats are open together for Vicki and me.

Vicki says grace, and everyone begins serving and passing the meal. She insists we eat as much as we want. I'm pleased to see glass cups filled with iced tea. The beef stew is delicious, served with fresh vegetables from the garden. Priscilla chats with two little blonde girls beside her. Vicki notices and explains they're her daughters. Their father died suddenly, and after moving west, they had no one to support them. Priscilla needed time to adjust, but time was a luxury she didn't have.

The girls seem happy here. I wish them all the best, including Priscilla. After dinner, Priscilla and Matilda clear the table and put away the food. Vicki moves to the piano and plays hymns, which she says are based on the Bible. Everyone sings for about thirty minutes, then Vicki reads from the Bible for another thirty.

Once the children head upstairs, I'm struck by how smoothly Vicki runs everything. Matilda and Priscilla follow, and I excuse myself to my guest room. There, I see Oscar eating beef from a bowl on the floor. I'd forgotten about him and felt relieved Vicki fed him, even though she hadn't wanted to bring him inside. She must have served two portions, thinking Octavius was a cat.

The room is small but cozy, with a floral quilt on a twin bed against the back wall and an armoire on the front wall. A wash basin and pitcher sit on a stand beside the bed. A gold-framed painting of flowers hangs above it. A Bible rests on the bed as I place my luggage by the armoire. I take out the ether device Ollie returned and examine it. It's locked, possibly DNA-activated. All I can see are two coordinates on the screen.

I notice the device has a button to reverse the coordinates, along with the enter button. I can only use the two coordinates interchangeably—one for my bedroom and one in front of Vicki's house. Realizing Damien had programmed the coordinates outside Vicki's house, I begin to wonder why. Why was my home the second coordinate? Were Ms. Collins and Professor Wendall planning to kill me and use the portal to return to the location in front of Vicki's orphanage? The real question is why. And Matilda's strange object looks a lot like a modern contact lens case.

I notice Octavius has changed back into himself, wearing his tuxedo and sitting on the bed, watching Oscar lick his paws and lips after the beef meal. I show the device to Octavius and ask what he thinks. He agrees it's DNA-locked, but notes we have the coordinates for home, which he stores in his memory. I think to myself it won't help much unless we figure out how to use it to get back.

I get ready for bed while Octavius returns to his charging pad. I remind him that the pad will last a few months, but needs to be recharged by an electrical outlet. Octavius agrees that we should stay here for a few days to be safe, as Ms. Collins and Professor Wendall might still be at our home.

We go to bed. Oscar sleeps beside me, and Octavius hides in a drawer in the armoire in case someone walks in while he's charging. The night is quiet and peaceful. I drift off to sleep, hearing Oscar snore as I turn onto my side.

I WAKE to the sound of Vicki and Priscilla in the kitchen. After checking on Octavius, I get dressed and step out.

Vicki looks up from her work. I smile. "Good morning."

"Good morning," she replies warmly.

"I can help with breakfast," I offer.

"That's sweet," she says, "but it's not necessary today."

"I could make the biscuits," I insist, glancing around for a mix.

One of the little boys nearby notices me searching. "What are you looking for?" he asks.

"I'm looking for biscuit mix."

He grins. "All the biscuit stuff is over there on the stand."

I follow his gaze and spot the ingredients—milk, flour, and a few others I don't immediately recognize. There's baking powder, sugar, salt, and butter laid out neatly.

"Oh, I was looking for a mix," I say with a smile.

"There isn't a mix for biscuits," the boy replies. "You have to combine the ingredients."

The little boy looks at me and asks how I don't know how to cook as an adult. I freeze, feeling useless. Vicki steps in and says, "That's enough. She can cook where she's from." I look at him and boldly say, "I'm from Illinois." Matilda walks in and gives me a curious look. The boy continues, "They must be weird in Illinois." Matilda laughs, and Vicki shoots her a disapproving glare.

Vicki turns back to the boy. "Play outside, Philip," she says.

He leaves, and Matilda lingers, clearly eavesdropping while pretending to stay busy. Vicki seems to notice but says nothing, continuing her work with minimal conversation to avoid encouraging her.

Vicki shows me how to make the biscuits using the ingredients and the wood stove. Breakfast is delicious and full of flavor. I think to myself, I could get used to this. During the meal, Matilda keeps glancing at me, and I get the sense I should keep Octavius close and my luggage locked.

After breakfast, Vicki asks if I'd like to help with her seamstress work. I agree, saying I'd be happy to. I remember I have a small purse in my luggage that I can carry Octavius in while I help. I'm actually curious to see how the process works.

CHAPTER 4

The house quiets as the children gather in the living room for class with Priscilla, the orphanage teacher. I expect to head to a room and start learning how to make clothes, but instead, Vicki asks me to get ready to go into town. She says she needs to run a few errands first. I'm surprised but agree—it'll be good to see the town anyway.

Back in the guest room, I find Oscar sprawled contentedly on the bed, licking his paws after breakfast. I grab my cream-colored crochet purse, tuck Octavius inside, and tie my long brown hair into a ponytail; it hasn't been washed since yesterday. Then I head to the front door. Vicki is already there, looking slightly upset, though I can't tell why. I try to stay pleasant; she's doing her best to help me.

We walk north along the old dirt road in front of the house. Vicki is quiet, lost in thought, until she finally says, "I know where you're from." I cough and ask what she means.

"I know you're from the future," she says. "Because I know a lady named Ms. Collins—the third widow staying with us, or so we're told. I know a lot right now because they underestimate me. They think I'm stupid, just because I'm from the past. They think they're so superior."

I stop and stare at her. "What do you mean by all of this?"

Vicki explains she overheard Ms. Collins and Matilda talking at night, when they thought everyone was upstairs. Sometimes, I'd stay in the guest room alone for a bit to escape the crowd—reading, drawing, just being quiet. They didn't know I was there, and that night, they were speaking loudly. They talked about the Ether device and time travel. And worse things, Desiree. Much worse.

I was stunned. I asked Vicki why she trusted me.

"Because Ms. Collins described you," she said. "She mentioned a woman named Desiree at the museum in Sanctuary. Long brunette hair, green eyes, slim build—not short or tall. She said you had limited access to the Ether device and that, if you got hold of it, you'd know who to look for."

I just stood there, unable to speak.

My voice trembles. "What's the worst part about all this?" I ask.

Vicki turns to me, her gaze steady. She says she knows about the nuclear war and what came after. What most people don't realize is that the Others took some of the rebels and created half-breeds. That's one reason the rebels no longer welcome outsiders. The crossbreeds look human—no mutations—but their eyes are magenta.

Vicki looks at me and says, "I could tell Matilda knows who you are."

I freeze. That explains Matilda's hostility, which had always seemed so unwarranted. It also doesn't help that I lack the skills to handle most household tasks in this era. Vicki says she's helping me because she wants to stop them. Their goal isn't just control in my time—they want to dominate all of history. To rewrite it. She says we need to start planning.

We've walked a long way and are almost to the town. It looks exactly like something from an old western film. But the smell of horse manure catches me off guard. Wooden and adobe buildings line the street, joined by a long, covered porch that stretches along both sides. Stagecoaches roll past, larger and more imposing than I imagined. As I take it all in, I suddenly realize the smell has been lingering for a while. I glance down and see that I've stepped in manure with my right boot.

While I'm staring in dismay, a voice behind me says, "That's my dress you have on."

I turn to see a woman eyeing the outfit I'm wearing. We stand there awkwardly in the middle of the street, unsure of what to say next.

Vicki steps in. "You could have come by anytime to get it, so don't take it out on my guest."

I respond quickly. "You must be Raquel."

She looks offended, scoffs, and walks off without a word.

Vicki calls after her. "You're welcome anytime to come and get your stuff."

I watch as Raquel disappears into the crowd on the covered porch. I can tell she's in a lot of pain by her demeanor, so I turn to Vicki and ask what happened. She sighs and lowers her head. She explains that her sister was offered a lucrative job serving drinks at a bar that seemed like a good opportunity. It turned out to be more of a gambling club for elite men. Vicki says she warned her sister that this wasn't how they were raised and that those men might expect more than just drinks being served. Raquel thought Vicki was being judgmental and not trying to understand how a short-term job could offer long-term financial stability. Vicki told her that God has a plan for her life and to pray and seek His will and purpose.

I respond, "I could tell Raquel didn't take your advice." Vicki looks down and says nothing.

We walk a little farther and pass an alley where, out of the corner of my eye, I catch a flash of Damien. I turn to look, but no one is there—only a tall pile of animal feed bags stacked high enough for someone to hide behind.

Just then, I hear Ollie's voice: "Good morning, Miss Desiree."

I look over at him and smile as he smiles back. He keeps his gaze on me, then suddenly asks if I'd like to join him for tea at the Corner Cafe just ahead. I glance at Vicki, and she smiles, so I know she approves. I agree, and we all head that way.

As we walk, I begin to wonder why Ollie wasn't surprised to see me emerge from a portal—and what that might mean. I have a feeling Vicki is holding something back, especially given Ollie's reaction. For now, I believe Vicki is more on my side than Matilda or Miss Collins. I also started to think I was right—Matilda did have a contact case with her.

The restaurant is charming, with dark cream lace curtains and matching lace tablecloths. It's small but cozy. I like the tan adobe walls and the low ceiling. A few paintings of floral tea sets hang on the walls. I think it's a sweet touch for a tea cafe to feature paintings of tea sets instead of the usual floral arrangements in vases.

Ollie lets me choose the table, and I head to the back corner, facing the window. I have no idea what the cafe offers, so I ask for a menu. Before I get a response, Ollie glances up at the waitress who has appeared beside us and orders black tea, along with two of each of the best fresh pastries they have at the moment. The waitress smiles and walks off.

I NOTICE that Ollie and Vicki aren't saying much to each other, so I start asking Ollie about his life. He believes he leads a simple life, mainly focused on the family business.

Just then, my purse—which I had laid on the table behind me—bounces. Ollie notices and informs me that it's moving. Horrified, I say it must be a bug inside, so I try to squish it. When it moves again, I excuse myself and step outside to deal with it.

Once outside, I hear Octavius say, "We have got to get Oscar and get out of here. It's obvious Matilda knows who we are and has informed Ms. Collins of our whereabouts."

I agree that we need to leave, but the question is where. I tell Octavius I don't think we can go back just yet, but we do need to find another place to stay as soon as possible. I let him know I'm heading back inside and that he needs to stay still until I can return him to the guest room.

Back inside the Corner Cafe, I sit down again.

I can tell Ollie is lonely—I see the same loneliness in myself back home. I work, take care of Oscar, and tend to my front porch garden. I start to feel sad thinking about home. I loved my job at the museum, but I struggled to maintain a good balance between my career and personal life.

The waitress returns with a serving tray holding teacups, a kettle, and the pastries. After we finish, Ollie says he'll be there for dinner on Friday. He pays the bill and says goodbye.

Vicki asks if we want to visit any shops before heading back to the orphanage.

. . .

I START LOOKING AROUND, remembering I don't have any money for 1880 anyway. Still, I want to visit a general store and see what's inside. The thought of exploring the groceries and household items sparks my curiosity —after all, I'm an archaeologist working for a museum.

Just then, we hear shouting and turn to see Raquel arguing with a group of men under the covered porch nearby. They're yelling that she'd better bring it with her next time. Raquel, clearly distressed, keeps insisting they talk to Lenny. Vicki storms over, and for a moment, I think she's about to punch the man closest to Raquel. Instead, she cuts in sharply, telling them to keep moving. The men back off, but not without a final warning—they say she'd better have it, or else.

I step away to give Vicki and Raquel some space. When Vicki returns, I can tell she's upset. She says we should head back to the orphanage. The general store will have to wait.

Back at the house, I set down my purse with Octavius still inside. I peek in and see a miniature version of him waving at me. I'm about to go to my room when Vicki stops me, asking if I have one of those "hologram thing-ma-do-dads." Caught off guard, I nod and explain that his name is Octavius. I let her peek inside my purse, and her face lights up.

"He's adorable," she says.

I take Octavius out and place him on the couch. He instantly jumps up and starts dancing, showing off his moves in his tiny tuxedo. Vicki laughs, clearly charmed. I find myself wondering how she even knows about technology like this.

Suddenly, we hear music. I turn and see Octavius hopping across the piano keys, playing a quirky rendition of "Puttin' on the Ritz." Vicki watches, completely entertained.

Then, as if to top it all off, Octavius climbs onto Oscar and rides him around the living room. Vicki claps with delight. The grandfather clock chimes noon.

"We should start dinner," she says. "The children and Priscilla will be back soon."

She tells me lunch will be simple today—bread, butter, and grape jam with milk.

We head into the kitchen to prepare. Vicki pulls out a loaf of bread she baked earlier that morning, slices it, and places the pieces in a woven basket for the table. She sets out plates and glasses, then heads out back to the root cellar to fetch the butter and jam, ready to serve once everyone returns.

We hear footsteps approaching, and Octavius quickly darts into the guest room with Oscar. Philip opens the door, carrying the butter and a jar of grape jam. The rest of the group follows behind, and we all gather around the dining table. Vicki says grace, and then we enjoy the simple bounty of bread, butter, and jam.

After lunch, the children head off to do their chores while Vicki begins prepping for supper. I ask what we'll be having on Friday. She smiles and says not to worry—it's going to be special. With a spark of excitement, she announces, "Meatloaf and mashed potatoes." Her enthusiasm is contagious, and I find myself looking forward to it.

I retreat to the guest room for a while to check on Oscar and Octavius. Everything is calm. Octavius is reading a miniature holographic book from a solid blue wingback chair. Oscar is on the floor, batting around a real ball of yarn Vicki left for him yesterday.

I realize Matilda hasn't been around since lunch. A thought nags at me— could she have an Ether device? And if so, how many are out there?

Meanwhile, Vicki sets to work on Ollie's order for Friday. I can tell she wants to finish it alone, especially after what happened earlier in town. I decide to pass the time quietly. I flip through the Bible again and read a few chapters from Genesis. Later, I make tea and feel a wave of homesickness wash over me. Oscar appears and nudges my leg, asking for attention. I scratch the top of his head, and his soft purring brings comfort. Feeling a bit more at ease, I let him out for a little while—there's no litter box in the house, after all.

We have porridge for dinner. Afterward, Vicki leads the children in singing hymns and reading more from the Bible. The warmth of the tradition settles in me, and I find myself looking forward to it again tomorrow night.

Matilda still hasn't returned, and night has fallen. Vicki plans to lock the doors at 9:00 PM. After that, if Matilda isn't back, she'll have to hope someone hears her knocking. There's no electric doorbell here.

Friday has arrived, and I'm looking forward to seeing Ollie tonight—and to meatloaf for dinner. I can tell it's a special day, as the children's chores are focused on tidying up the living room and dining room. Philip is under the dining table, dusting but also sneaking in playful moments with the other children when no adults are watching. He's always been fascinated by a ceramic horse Vicki keeps on the bookshelf—a small tan horse rearing back, front legs kicking, head tilted and mouth open. It's charming and clearly one of a kind. Vicki made it from clay her father brought home years ago from a riverbank in California. He had gone west briefly during the gold rush but came back empty-handed. Vicki loves making pottery, but out here in the desert, clay is hard to come by.

As Philip scoots around under the table, he accidentally knocks over an expensive candle holder near the piano. Out of nowhere, Matilda appears and snaps at him to be careful, saying that if he keeps being so clumsy, no one will ever want him. Philip bursts into tears. Vicki comes in and asks what's going on. I explain, but Matilda turns to me instead.

"And what have you done all week to help out around the house?" she asks coldly.

I hesitate.

"Exactly what I thought," she says. "You're useless—and Philip is too clumsy to be a mommy's boy anyway."

Philip screams, "I have a mom!" and runs to Vicki, sobbing.

Vicki's face tightens. Philip clutches at her, crying, "You are my mommy!"

Her voice trembles slightly as she walks over to the bookshelf, picks up the ceramic horse, and kneels beside him.

"For now," she says softly, "I'm our mom. I don't know if that will change. But you'll always have a home here."

Philip's face lights up as he hugs the ceramic horse tightly.

Vicki stands and calmly asks Matilda to come outside to talk. As Matilda turns to leave, she bumps into me and mutters, "Watch out, idiot," under her breath. I say nothing, but I watch through the window as she and Vicki argue outside. When Vicki turns to head back inside, Matilda makes a rude gesture behind her.

Vicki returns without a word, goes upstairs, and comes back down with a laundry bag and a few books. She carries them outside and hands them to Matilda. Matilda throws down the bag, grabs the books, and walks off.

I found it strange that Matilda didn't take her clothes with her, but then again, who knows? Maybe she isn't even from this time period. I can't shake the feeling that she orchestrated everything—to throw her weight around the house and assert control. She always acted as though she was above everyone else here. I doubt she expected Vicki to kick her out so soon. Still, I don't think she would've revealed much more about the Others' plans anyway. And it's clear that Ms. Collins isn't coming back with me.

Vicki asks me to help with dinner while Priscilla is out back gathering potatoes and herbs. When she returns, we work together in the kitchen to prepare the meal.

I set the table and make lemonade. A little while later, I hear the children run to the door and open it, chatting excitedly. Priscilla joins them, gently steering them into the living room to give Ollie space and a bit of peace.

I step into the room to greet him. He's brought a bouquet of blanket flowers—bright and cheerful, with red petals, yellow tips, and golden centers. I take them to the kitchen and place them in a vase. Vicki watches me arrange them, smiling, and together, we carry the meal into the dining room.

Once everyone is seated, I notice Ollie has chosen the seat right beside mine. Vicki asks him to say grace, and then we begin. Philip has brought the ceramic horse figurine with him and quietly plays with it while eating.

After dinner, we gather in the living room to sing songs around the piano while Vicki plays. The evening feels warm and full. Still, I find it odd that Ollie never asks questions—not even about seeing me come through a portal. Maybe he didn't notice. Or maybe he's waiting for the right time to say something. We haven't had a private conversation yet, so it's hard to tell.

Before leaving, Vicki gives him his order. He thanks her, then turns to me.

"Will you be at church on Sunday?" he asks.

"I will," I say.

He smiles and heads out. It's almost dark.

Back in the guest room, I find three new dresses laid out neatly on the bed. Curious, I search for Vicki in the living room. She explains that Ollie bought them—for me—so I could have proper dresses of my own.

I return to my room and study them closely. They remind me of Raquel's dress, but these are true prairie dresses, each one beautiful. One is white with a pink floral pattern. Another is cream and black in a small check. The third is a soft, dust rose color. Beside them sits a pair of Victorian-style light brown leather Granny boots with small heels.

I decide to set the dresses aside for the night and spend some quiet time with Oscar and Octavius. I thumb through the Bible again and feel a deeper connection than before. For the first time in a while, I pray—thanking God for bringing Vicki and Ollie into my life. I go to sleep feeling content, delighted.

Sunday arrives, and I choose the dusty rose dress and the new boots for church. Almost everyone is already at the front door, waiting for Priscilla and her two daughters. When they come downstairs, Priscilla smiles and tells me the dress looks beautiful. We head out together.

The walk is a fair distance, but soon the church comes into view. It's a wooden building with an open steeple and a visible bell. At the top of the steeple is an arched roof with a large wooden cross mounted above it. A small porch with seven steps leads up to the entrance, which is flanked by two long, slim arched windows—one on each side of the door.

As we approach, I scan the crowd, looking for Ollie. Philip and the two other boys run ahead, full of energy, rushing into the building to find their friends. Vicki carries her Bible, something I hadn't thought to bring. I'd been more focused on looking nice for Ollie. I make a mental note to get mine next Sunday. I do have my purse, though—and, of course, Octavius.

Inside, the church is simple but welcoming. Wooden pews fill the room, leading up to a pulpit at the front. An upright piano sits off to the left, and a large wooden cross is mounted on the wall behind the pulpit.

Ollie is in the back row. When he hears the door open, he turns and stands to greet us. He shifts over to make room, and I sit beside him while Vicki and Priscilla take the seats next to us.

Ollie leans over and tells me that Vicki likes to sit in the back so she can keep an eye on the children up front. I smile and say That sounds exactly like something she'd do. As the choir begins to sing, I thank him for the dresses. He shrugs it off, saying it was nothing, for a friend of Vicki's.

As the sermon begins, I listen closely, so much so that I forget about Ollie sitting next to me. I feel Octavius shift around a bit inside my purse, but no one seems to notice.

A quiet cough draws my attention to the left side of the church. I glance over and see Raquel sitting with another woman, who I assume is a friend. The woman, a Native American, seems lost in thought. I wonder why Vicki doesn't go over to say hello, but decides not to ask—it's not really my place.

After the sermon, I spot Raquel and her friend rising to leave. I offer a polite smile. Raquel gives me a faint one in return before turning back to her conversation.

We head out, and as we walk, Vicki calls the children over and gives each of them a penny to spend at the candy store. I have a feeling Ollie gave her the money on Friday—along with the dresses and shoes.

The children light up with excitement, running down the street despite their hand-me-down clothes and worn shoes, some too tight, others slipping off.

Ollie turns to me. "Would you like to come to Wednesday night Bible study?"

"That sounds nice," I say.

He nods with a small smile.

"I'll see you then," he says, heading off down the street.

I glance back as he walks away and catch him looking back at me.

Without thinking, I blurt out, "Why didn't you say hello to Raquel?"

Vicki sighs. "I'm giving her space. She needs to make her own decisions." Her voice softens. "I'm praying every day she'll come back home—and return to the Lord."

Just then, Priscilla catches up with us, having paused to chat after church. She falls into step beside us and starts talking about upcoming church events. Vicki walks on in silence.

CHAPTER 5

I wake early the next morning and decide it's time to return Raquel's dress. I slip on the white floral one instead and pack the green dress under my arm. Octavius goes in my purse, as always, and Oscar follows me to the door, tail wagging. I let him come along. The cool morning air feels good, and I welcome the quiet time to think. I'll need to go home soon. What will I do when I get there?

When I reach town, I head toward the spot where I last saw Raquel. Vicki mentioned where she works, so I started searching nearby. Oscar slows, sniffing around the covered porch of one of the buildings. I've found it. I give him a quick scratch behind the ears and let him stay outside.

Inside, I find an expansive room with several tables scattered about and a bar lining the back wall—likely a place for card games and gambling—no sign of Raquel.

A murmur catches my attention from a cracked door to the left. I step closer, still holding the green dress. Before I knock, I hear a man's voice.

"Raquel, please," he says. "I love you. I swear I'll pay you back soon—I just need a little more time."

Peeking through the narrow opening, I see him standing beside her. Raquel is seated at a vanity, brushing her hair. It looks like a dressing room for the waitresses.

Her voice is calm but firm. "You said that last time. And the time before that."

He shifts uneasily, glancing toward the door.

"You've borrowed a lot from me," she continues. "And you haven't paid back a single cent."

There's a pause.

"You only show up when you want something," Raquel says. "I haven't even met your friends or your family—not once in over a year."

The man doesn't respond. Raquel keeps brushing her hair, eyes focused straight ahead in the mirror.

Watching her now, I understand why everyone talks about Raquel. She's stunning—long auburn hair, light green eyes, a flawless smile. The man, with his dark hair and eyes, has a certain charm, but he's not worth the trouble. Not when he clearly doesn't care for her and is only using her. I don't understand how someone like her puts up with it. Doesn't she know she deserves better?

And then it hits me: this must be what Vicki was so angry about. Why did those men warn Raquel the other day? She was expected to cover his gambling debt. Or else.

I have a feeling that this man will vanish soon, leaving Raquel to face whatever comes next. I shift my weight, and the wooden floor creaks. The man snaps his head toward the door.

"Who's there?" he demands.

I freeze, holding my breath.

"I said, who's there?" His voice is sharper now.

I step back, heart pounding, unsure whether to bolt or stay. I don't want Raquel to know I overheard. Before I can make a decision, he moves toward the door.

I force a smile and sputter. "Oh, there you are, Raquel. I just came to return your dress."

He eyes me. "How long were you standing there?"

"I just arrived. You heard the floor squeak when I stepped in," I lie, hoping it sounds natural.

The man has the polished coldness of someone used to threats and manipulation. The longer I stand here, the more I believe Vicki was right. I hand Raquel the dress. She looks drained, her eyes heavy with defeat and a hint of fear.

"Thank you," she says softly, taking the dress.

The man steps closer, flashing a false smile. "Have a nice day." He nearly slams the door in my face, forcing me to step aside.

That's when it hits me: Raquel is in real danger. And I need to do something about it.

Outside, I find Oscar still sniffing the porch, blissfully unaware of the tension I'm carrying. I start heading back toward the orphanage, trying to gather my thoughts, when I hear a voice I instantly recognize. My stomach turns.

"Hello, Desiree. It's never a pleasure to see you," Damien sneers.

I'm in no mood for this. As I glance back, I hear footsteps. Ms. Collins and Professor Wendall are approaching. I bend to scoop up Oscar, ready to make a run for it, but then a better idea flashes into my mind.

"I just found a hundred dollars!" I shout. "Does it belong to anyone?"

About five men burst out of the Gentlemen's Club, knocking us over as they scramble to see where the money went. I dart into the dirt street and nearly run into a stagecoach as I head east. Up ahead, I spot a train station with an engine already smoking, ready to depart. Panic sets in—I have no money. What am I going to do?

When I glance back, I see Ms. Collins and Professor Wendall following. Oddly, Damien hasn't joined them. He lingers near the alley by the Gentlemen's Club, probably to keep a low profile. His gray coloring makes him stand out.

Oscar is tucked under my arm, but he's had enough of the chaos and starts squirming. I race into the station and spot Ollie standing with a ticket in hand. He hears me coming, notices the crowd chasing behind, and quickly hands me the ticket. I don't hesitate. I sprint to the train and jump aboard. Ms. Collins and Professor Wendall stop short—I assume because there are too many people around now.

I collapse into an empty passenger car, still clutching Oscar, who begins growling in protest. I set him down and clutch my purse instead. Through the window, I see Ollie running along the platform, then jumping onto the train. He finds me and sits down beside us.

"I like to be around you," Ollie says.

We fall into a quiet stretch. I sit with the ticket clenched in my hand while Oscar begins exploring the car. I ask where we're headed, and Ollie tells me Chapel Hill. He has business there—something about a family dispute with another rancher.

"Thank you for helping me," I say.

He smiles and looks out the window, adding that when the conductor comes around, he'll buy a new ticket. I find it strange that he doesn't ask who those people were or why they were after me. I think he enjoys my company, but I also suspect he knows more about Damien than he's letting on.

My purse starts to move again. Ollie notices and offers to get rid of the bug for me, reaching toward it. I scream and tell him it's fine—I'll handle it. He grins and tugs on the purse as I pull back. Suddenly, a miniature Octavius clings to the brim of the bag, hanging on for dear life. Ollie jumps back in surprise.

"What is that?" he asks.

I sigh and glance at him. "He's a computer hologram. Or image."

Ollie squints. "What's a computer?"

I try to explain. "It's kind of like a train—mechanical. But it's for information and communication instead of travel."

He nods slowly, clearly turning it over in his head, then begins peppering me with questions about Octavius.

Octavius now sits between us on the seat. Ollie's clearly impressed by how human he seems. I explain that he's programmed that way—at which point Octavius bristles.

"I'm more human than humans are," he declares.

The train starts to slow as we approach the next station. Ollie asks if I'm hungry, suggesting we grab something to eat before he heads to his appointment with the other rancher. I hold a nervous Oscar close as we step off the train.

Ollie motions toward a nearby restaurant. As we walk, I keep a tight grip on Oscar. But when we reach the door, the hostess frowns at him and tells me, "That flea bag can't come inside."

"He might get lost," I say, not quite pleading.

Ollie steps in. "It's okay. There's another café nearby. Bit of a walk, though."

It is a bit of a walk, but I quickly see why Ollie suggested it. The café is outdoors, shaded by a vast canopy that softens the morning sun. We choose a table away from the other diners, and a waitress comes over with menus. She smiles at Oscar, offering him a bowl of water and a plate of chicken scraps from the kitchen.

Ollie and I both ordered eggs, bacon, biscuits, and gravy. The waitress brings the orange juice first, followed by the tea. I feel comfortable here. Safe. Oscar's relaxed, and even Octavius seems to like Ollie.

As we eat, I notice a familiar man walking with Raquel's friend from church. He was the one with Raquel before. They don't seem to be arguing —just deep in conversation. Ollie follows my gaze, curious.

I explain what happened that morning when I tried to return Raquel's dress to her at work.

Ollie tells me he's no one important, just someone who picks up second-hand knowledge from the gamblers' conversations. Sometimes, politicians or wealthy men come to drink and watch poker games, and he's been known to sell information he overhears.

It seems that's what he believes the two people we saw are discussing— something he caught wind of at a card game. I watch as they stand talking in the middle of the street, then part ways. The man heads back toward the train station, while she walks in the opposite direction, leaving town.

Ollie notices my curiosity and offers to walk in her direction after we finish eating, so I can see where she went. I get the feeling he knows more about their conversation than he's letting on. Under the table, Oscar licks his paws in the cool shade, clearly enjoying himself.

I still haven't adjusted to the heat or the wind. I'm used to climate-controlled conditions—no rain, no gusts of wind—under the dome of the city-state. Being out here, exposed to the elements, feels unpredictable. There's a kind of vulnerability in it.

As we leave the café, Ollie pays for the meal. Just outside, a man approaches him, looking urgent. I catch enough to know it's about the family ranch—something went wrong with the other rancher this morning.

Ollie's face tightens. He asks the man why he didn't wait for him to arrive at the meeting. The man, now looking at me, asks who I am.

"I'm Desiree, from Illinois," I say.

He doesn't look impressed. Instead, he starts arguing with Ollie, trying to justify why they went ahead without him. Ollie glances at his watch. "The meeting wasn't supposed to start for another thirty minutes. You two started early and made a mess of things."

The man mutters something, backs off, and then leaves.

This has become a real problem for Ollie. And I can't help but feel a little responsible. If I hadn't gone to return Raquel's dress this morning, he wouldn't have taken me out to breakfast. He would've gone straight to meet his brother and the other rancher as planned, even if they had arrived ahead of schedule.

Ollie says there's no longer an appointment, so we might as well see where Raquel's friend went. We start down the dirt road in the direction she took. The sun presses warm against my head, and I begin to wonder how far she actually walked.

Oscar trails behind us, weaving in and out of the brush, exploring on his own. Ollie is quiet, clearly upset, and deep in thought. As we walk, guilt creeps in. I wish I hadn't gone to see Raquel today. Maybe then none of this would have gotten in the way.

CHAPTER 6

The sun bears down on us as we follow the dirt road, its heat relentless. I've never sweated so much in my life. I make a mental note to find a sunhat or parasol as soon as I can. When we finally reach the top of a hill, we stop. Beyond it, the land stretches out into an empty desert. I'm about to suggest we turn back when I spot a woman kneeling far off in the distance.

I think it's Raquel's friend. I gesture for Ollie to check with me. We haven't gone far when we hear her crying—calling out to God for help, pleading for her tribe. It's raw and uncomfortable to witness. She doesn't know we're here.

She's praying because the government plans to force her tribe off its land. She learned this from Frank. I assume that's the same man swindling Raquel. I've never met a Frank I liked.

I feel helpless, just standing there, listening as she weeps and pleads. Oscar starts walking toward her, and Ollie and I try to call him back. She hears us then, startled, and turns around. The moment she sees us, her expression shifts—embarrassment first, then defensiveness.

I want to say something, anything, but the words don't come easily. I tell her I'd like to help, that I'll do whatever I can. She grows angry, telling me I don't understand—that I don't share her burden. She means I'm not

Native American, that I don't know what it's like to be forced onto a reservation.

I ask her name, hoping to show some respect so that I can pray for her as well. She hesitates, then says she goes by June among non-Native Americans.

"Okay," I say gently. "I'll pray for you, June."

Oscar edges forward again, tail wagging, trying to coax her into a moment of comfort. But she doesn't reach for him. He eventually turns and trots back to me. I nod to Ollie and start to walk away. June wants to be alone.

We head back down the dirt road toward the train station when something on the far side catches my eye. I point it out to Ollie, and we decide to take a closer look. From a distance, it looks like a bundle of white fabric. As we approach, we realize it's an overturned wagon. The canvas cover is worn and slightly torn, but the structure itself still seems sound. Judging by the soil gathered around it, it's been here a while.

Who would leave a perfect wagon out here? I ask aloud. Ollie says it was probably ambushed—that's usually how wagons end up like this.

"Ambushed by who?" I ask.

He shrugs. "It's not called the Wild West for nothing. Could've been robbers, maybe a run-in with Natives—or even a rogue bull from a grazing herd that wandered through while the wagon was passing."

I glance around, taking in the emptiness. It hits me just how isolated it all feels. One wrong move out here, and you're on your own. Still, I don't think anyone was hurt. There's no sign of violence—just a lone, empty wagon left behind.

An idea strikes me. I tell Ollie I need a break from all of this, and maybe I could use the wagon to carry my luggage and pick up some supplies. He doesn't hesitate. Says he'll come too. He has a horse at his ranch, which allows him to gather what we need.

Ollie adds that he has family out in California and suggests we head that way. They live in a house made from a giant tree stump, he says. After the lumberjacks cut down the sequoias, the stumps can be hollowed out and roofed to make homes. The way he describes it, it sounds strange and fascinating—and honestly, I'd like to see it.

Just then, my purse starts to wiggle again. I let Octavius out, and he bolts for the wagon, scrambling all over it with excitement. Oscar joins in, tail wagging, sniffing his way around the old wooden frame.

I ask Ollie what tribe June is from. He tells me, "The Yellow Falcon Tribe." Curious and unsettled, I ask Octavius to look up their history, especially regarding any forced removals. After a pause, he informs me that in about two months, the government will attempt to relocate the tribe to a reservation—one they refuse to go to.

"What happened?" I ask quietly.

Octavius hesitates. Then he says the government and the tribe fought. No survivors from the Yellow Falcon Tribe were recorded. Their remains were left scattered in the desert. No one was there to bury them.

The news stuns me. I stand frozen, the devastation settling in, when I hear footsteps behind us. I turn to see two Native American men, maybe in their mid-twenties, watching us. Their expressions are tense. They've listened to what Octavius just said, and they don't look pleased.

One of them speaks first. "We came to see what you're doing here."

The other points to Octavius. "What is that? And how does it know that about our tribe?"

Ollie glances at me, clearly uncertain. My mind races, but I can't think of a single thing to say that will make this right. The men keep staring, their unease turning to suspicion.

"I think it's best you leave," I say, edging toward the road. "We're going back to the train station."

They don't move. Now they want more details about the tribe's future, about what's coming. I shake my head. "You've heard enough. Let us pass."

Suddenly, the first man lets out a sharp, unfamiliar sound. A call of some kind. When he repeats it, I realize it's a signal for backup. He's calling for others.

Without hesitation, I pull out the Ether device and scan the coordinates. The current setting shows my home in Sanctuary. I quickly press the reverse coordinate button, and it shifts—Vicki's Orphanage now displayed.

I scoop up Oscar and Octavius and turn to Ollie. "Hold on to me," I tell him.

He stares at me, confused. "What? Why?"

"Just do it. Now."

Still unsure, he grabs my arm. I take a breath and hit Enter.

I feel the pulse of energy again, followed by a blinding flash of light as everything around us grinds to a halt. I think Ollie's gripping me tightly now as we're pulled through the portal, the air around us stale and still. Then it's over—we've landed. I look up and see the orphanage straight ahead as I push myself off the ground. Ollie and Oscar remain where they are for a moment, and Octavius looks visibly shaken.

"I THINK we're starting to mess up the time continuum," Octavius says. "Those men saw me. They know what the timeline was supposed to be. And they saw the portal. Who knows what they'll do now? But they definitely saw me, and they're not the kind of men who back down."

I have to agree. I'm no longer sure if 1880 is safer than 2280. If I hadn't had the Ether device with me—if they had seen Octavius without it—we might not have escaped. One of them had already called for backup.

I turn to Ollie. "We need to get out of here. Now."

He looks at me and asks where I'm from. I tell him Illinois—just not this version of it.

"When exactly?" he asks.

"2280."

He blinks. "The future is

"No," I say. "The future is 1880."

There's a long silence.

I go on. "There are people from my time chasing me. They want the Ether device back, but I used it to escape something almost identical to what just happened. They want to use it to rewrite history and take control of the world."

Ollie stares at the orphanage, lost in thought. Then he stands and says, "We need to stick to the plan and leave as soon as possible." He wants to get the horse now and asks me to grab a few supplies from the house.

I hesitate and tell him I think we're rushing. A good night's rest would help, and it might be smarter to head out at first light.

Ollie shakes his head. "We need to leave now." He tells me he recognized the man from June's tribe—the one who first approached us. His name is Red Fang, and he's known for being petty and vengeful. There have even been accusations of him setting fires when things don't go his way.

I stand there, thinking through everything. It's happening so fast. After a moment, I nod and start getting my things together. I hope Vicki isn't home. I don't want to say goodbye—not now, not like this.

Inside, I hurry to the guest room, grab my suitcase and the clothes Ollie got me, and run back out. Before leaving, I snatch the Bible from the bed. Vicki might be upstairs or out of the house entirely. I was only inside for two minutes. She'll understand later, once she learns I was in trouble with the Others.

As Ollie and I walk away, dragging our suitcases behind us, I glance back at the orphanage. I carry Oscar under one arm, Octavius nestled in my purse. I feel helpless. Hungry. I want this all to be over.

This time, we take a different road, one that forks to the right. Ollie says we're not going into town—we're heading to his ranch. He wants to avoid attention, especially since people talk a lot around here.

After a long walk, a beautiful Victorian home comes into view. I get the sense Ollie's family must be the wealthy benefactors who donated the house to the orphanage. Off to the side, there's a fenced-in area with a few horses.

Ollie heads toward it and calls out, "Lightning."

A striking black horse, sleek and muscular, trots up to the fence. Ollie tells me to wait as he retrieves a lasso from a hook on the wall, loops it around the horse, and leads it through the gate. He brings Lightning to the barn and attaches him to a covered buggy—simple, but roomy enough for the two of us.

I glance at the buggy and then at Ollie. "What about your clothes?" I ask.

"Do I need clothes from the future here?" he replies with a smile.

I shake my head. "No."

With that, Ollie goes into the house to pack a few essentials. He returns with a leather travel bag and instructs me to pack my clothes in it. I keep my undergarments and socks in my own suitcase, then hand the rest over. He also grabs some food supplies and more money before we set out.

I asked Ollie why he hadn't mentioned having a buggy. He says he kept it to himself because he was forming a plan. The abandoned wagon had inspired his idea to go to California. That wagon would've been ideal—bigger and better for the trip—but it's too dangerous to try retrieving it now.

Then I get an idea: maybe we should take the train. It can't be any worse than traveling by buggy, and what we'd spend on food for a long journey might equal the cost of a train ticket. Ollie thinks about it and agrees. Neither of us thinks logically; we want to get away.

Ollie returns the food to the house, then takes our luggage to the barn and hides it. Most of the ranch hands are out grazing cattle, so it should be safe while we're gone. He puts Lightning back in the round corral, and we start walking toward town, Ollie carrying the travel bag.

He asks, "Are you hungry?"

I nod. "Let's stop at the corner café after we get our tickets."

Once in town, we head straight to the train station and map out a route to California. There's a train leaving in an hour—perfect timing.

We both feel more at ease as we walk toward dinner. But halfway there, I spot June back in town, standing with Frank in front of the Gentlemen's Club. They notice us, then quickly turn away when they realize I've seen them.

A bad feeling settles in my stomach.

I nudge Ollie. "Did you see that?"

"Yeah," he says, eyes narrowing. "Makes me wonder how much June knows about the Ether device now."

June watches us as we pass. At the Corner Café, we sit down and rest. The lemonade is crisp, and the lamb stew is warm and filling. Oscar eats leftover beef scraps. The meal is comforting. We pay and head out.

On the way back to the train station, a woman suddenly barrels into me from behind. She falls to the ground, making a scene, and accuses me of running into her. I'm stunned.

"You ran into me," I say. "From behind."

The hit was full force. My shoulder aches, and I know I'll bruise. I take a closer look at her. Something about her face, her posture—she reminds me of Matilda. Is it her in disguise?

Ollie helps the lady up and tells her she seems okay, then adds that we'll be on our way. She gives us a mincing glare and sits down on a bench under

43

the covered porch. As we walk away, I notice a satisfied grin on her face, and I begin to wonder what she did.

We board the train, showing the conductor our tickets as I carry Oscar under my arm. It feels good to sit down again—it's been a long day. The train pulls out of the station, and Ollie looks relieved that we're finally leaving Rocky Creek.

About thirty minutes into the ride, a woman walks into our passenger car. She seems odd, more interested in watching us than choosing a seat. I'm hoping nothing else happens today as she sits directly behind us in an otherwise empty car. I notice she has a travel bag with her. She remains seated while Ollie appears to rest, eyes shut, as I sit by the window, looking out.

My purse begins to shake again, and I peek inside as Octavius appears, motioning for me to come closer. I know he has something to tell me, so I glance around for a quiet place to talk. Just then, I hear a commotion outside as the train slows down significantly. Another noise comes from the passenger car behind us. I look out the window and see Native Americans on horseback surrounding the train. Have I just stepped into an old Western movie? My next question is, why would they be doing this? Then I see Red Fang through the window, and it starts to make sense. He sees me inside the passenger car.

The lady behind us suddenly stands up and says, in a gritty voice, "Hands up and reach for the sky. I've always wanted to say that."

Ollie and I slowly turn around to see her holding a gun, aimed straight at us. She looks quite pleased with herself. My purse starts moving again, and I whisper to Octavius that I'm a bit busy right now.

The noise outside keeps growing louder. Now Red Fang is at the window, watching us while we're being held at gunpoint by this mystery woman. So much for a quiet afternoon.

Red Fang pounds on the window when he spots me. Ollie looks at me and asks if the device is ready. I glance back, thinking, How can I get it out of my purse? The woman starts yelling at us not to move. I have no idea how we're going to get out of this as the train speeds down the track.

CHAPTER 7

The locomotive screams as we round a corner, the rails squeaking and the whistle blowing. The purse on the seat next to me begins to move again, and I hear Octavius calling for me. It jumps, falls to the floor, and I feel something brush against my leg. I glance at Ollie, who then looks past me toward the woman sitting behind us—the same one who held us at gunpoint earlier.

The next thing I know, Octavius is riding Oscar and about to leap at her. I scream, "No!" just as she looks down toward where the purse used to be. Suddenly, there's a loud thud, and the woman spins around and collapses just as Octavius and Oscar lunge at her.

Who hit her from behind? Octavius and Oscar land on the back of her seat. Octavius tries to say something quickly, but the train whistle blows again, cutting him off.

"We need to get out of here before she wakes up," Ollie says, glancing down.

He picks up the gun and slips it back into her travel bag.

"Why there?" I ask.

"She'll never expect to find it in her own bag," he replies.

I pause. "How do you think Red Fang found us?"

"Probably loose lips back at the train station," Ollie says. "Word travels fast when people don't know how to keep quiet."

We make our way toward the next passenger car, both for safety and to see what's going on. It's difficult to walk, as the train sways and hisses on its path.

I'd forgotten how to separate the passenger cars, and I have to climb over the hitch connecting them. I'm not sure how we'll manage this with Oscar and Octavius. Just then, I hear a loud bang and turn around—Red Fang has entered the passenger car through the front connecting door. Now the woman is waking up, and we're trapped in the back of the train with her as Red Fang slowly makes his way toward us.

I shout to him, "You're too late. She has the Ether device now!"

Red Fang confidently approaches her. Then, out of nowhere, she swings at him and clocks him hard. He goes down but quickly gets back up and tries to grab her travel bag. While they're fighting, Ollie says we have to jump. I look at him, unsure I heard right, and ask him to repeat it. He tells us again—we have to jump while they're distracted.

Ollie grabs my arm and scoops up Oscar as I grab Octavius and toss him into my purse. We all jump out through the back connecting door. Fortunately, the train had slowed to nearly a stop by the time we jumped. The Yellow Falcon tribe was attempting to block it by riding in front of the tracks.

The landing is rough—I fall and roll a little. My dress is dirty but not torn, and my purse with Octavius is intact. I have a few scratches on my legs and elbows. I glance over at Ollie, and he's also dusty and scraped up.

My purse starts shaking firmly as Octavius calls for me again. Ollie says we need to hide as the train passes by. We scramble into a ditch and wait to see if anyone from the ambush ahead is watching. No one seems to be around, so we stay low and move directly away from the tracks.

I ask Ollie what we're going to do now. He says he knows a place we can go out here. When I press him for details, he explains that most ranchers use federal land to graze their cattle, rotating the herds to prevent overgrazing.

"Are we going to hide out with ranchers?" I ask.

He looks at me and says, "Yes."

We move through rocky terrain and fields of patchy grass. I could really use a drink of water after all this walking under the relentless sun. Ollie tells me his family owns private property nearby with a few bunkhouses and a small cabin, one where my parents used to stay together.

I wonder if anyone from the ambush knows we've already left. I can almost picture their faces when they realize we're gone. My purse starts shaking again—Octavius is trying to get my attention. Just then, Ollie grabs my arm and points ahead. A long snake lies in the middle of the path. It's at least as long as I am tall, tan, with a brown diamond pattern across its body.

Ollie says it's a juvenile rattlesnake, and a large one at that. It doesn't seem threatened; instead, it sits still as if inviting us to step over it. Ollie doubles back a bit and takes a different path, saying he doesn't want to take any unnecessary risks. Sometimes, letting nature have its way is the smartest choice.

UP AHEAD, I see a few men on horseback dressed in old Western clothing and hats. I've now seen real-life cowboys. The men chat as they ride by, and I realize I've never been this close to a horse before. They're much larger in person than I had imagined.

It's strange, but for the first time, I truly feel like I'm in 1880. The cowboys nod to acknowledge us and continue on their way. I begin to feel the urge to ride a horse, too—or at least try.

Up ahead, Ollie points out the bunkhouse and cabin. I'm thrilled to hear this. All I want is a tall glass of water. I catch a smell on the wind—baked beans. And cornbread. My mouth starts to water. I hadn't realized how hungry I was.

After crossing the last hill, I can see the bunkhouses and the cabin in the distance. The bunkhouse on the right has a chimney with smoke curling up into the air.

Ollie walks up and knocks on the door. A man answers, dressed in traditional cowboy clothes. His face lights up when he sees Ollie.

"Well, if it ain't the boss man," he says cheerfully.

He invites us in and offers food. Ollie and I sit at a small table.

"We'd love to eat," I say.

The man ladles beans from a cast-iron pot hanging above the fireplace and fills two bowls. He sets them down in front of us, then points toward the cupboard.

"There's water here. Lemons and sugar in the cupboard if you want to make lemonade later."

He seems eager to head out and soon steps outside, leaving us alone.

I glance at Ollie. "What's your dream in life?"

He thinks for a moment. "Honestly, I haven't thought about it much. I've always worked for my family. I'm still young—I guess I haven't had the chance to dream about anything else."

He looks at me. "What about you? What's your dream?"

"I used to want exactly what I had," I say. "My dream was to be an archaeologist, work in a museum."

I pause. "But now, I'm not so sure. Lately, I've realized... I eat breakfast alone. I walk to the grocery store alone. I plan vacations alone."

Ollie studies me quietly. "Why don't you visit your family anymore?"

"They live far away," I say. "And besides... You can feel alone even in a crowd. My family has their own lives."

I hesitate, almost stopping there. But I go on.

"I guess I achieved what I once wanted. Now I'm trying to figure out what I want next—and how to get it."

Ollie pauses. "I do have a dream," he says quietly. "But it's kind of a small one. I've always wanted to fly in a hot air balloon."

I look at him and smile. "That's possible."

He shrugs. "I don't have the time right now—not with the family business. But one day, I feel it—I will fly in a hot air balloon."

After dinner, Ollie heads out to show me the cabin. Before I follow, I take one last look around the room. There's a fireplace on the west wall, two bunk beds across from it, a cupboard on the north wall, and a small table with four chairs in the center. Cast-iron pots sit at the base of the fireplace, and a small mantle clock rests in the middle. Beneath the table is a woven rug that catches my eye. It shows burros being led through the desert, colorful blankets on their backs like saddles. The people guiding them are laughing, dressed in bright Mexican clothing.

I motion to the rug. "Where did you get this?"

Ollie glances down. "I made it."

I take a step back, surprised. "You're really talented. You should think about tapestry weaving."

He shrugs again. "Out here, you either get good at making things or go without—unless you've got the money to buy everything at the general store, or something worth trading."

We walk toward the cabin, passing the second bunkhouse. In the distance, I spot a plateau mountain. The upper part looks jagged and foreboding. I wouldn't want to climb it.

The cabin looks smaller than the bunkhouses. Ollie opens the door to a cozy living room. There's a fireplace on the west wall and a cupboard on the north. A ladder on the east wall leads up to a loft with a bed and a small dresser.

The living room is furnished with two green velvet Victorian couches facing each other, a coffee table between them, and a tea cart nearby. A bookcase stands to the right. On the mantle sits another clock, flanked by tall sterling silver candlesticks, one at each end.

I imagine the cupboard holds beautiful dishes, and I'm sure the bed is comfortable. I'm glad we're not camping out, as we originally planned to do tonight. Ollie, still carrying the travel bag, sets it down on the table in front of the fireplace. He takes out his things and leaves the bag for me—he'll be sleeping in the unused second bunkhouse tonight.

He points out a sink beside the cupboard, along with a few kitchen cabinets. I glance over and see a porcelain sink. He tells me there's tea and other items for the evening, and I can heat water using the kettle at the fireplace. He adds that he'll stop by soon to light a fire if I'd like tea. Though the ranchers will be making their own later, he suggests I might prefer his. Then he leaves to look around the ranch while there's still plenty of daylight.

What can I do to pass the time? I remember bringing my Bible. I sit at the kitchen table and read for a while, then move to the couches, which are much more comfortable.

I'd forgotten about Oscar and Octavius, who're still in my purse. Now that I think of it, he's been unusually quiet. I check on them. Oscar got pork for dinner today. I call out for Octavius, but there's no answer—something about that feels off.

Just then, I hear a loud commotion outside. A group of people has gathered around the cabin, peering in through the windows. I hear Red Fang shouting, so I quickly grab my purse and Oscar.

My thoughts race—I need a plan. First, I have to find Ollie. I duck away from the windows and listen. Soon, I hear his voice, and I want to run to him. I leave Oscar hidden in the cabin and take my purse with me. I open the door to find Ollie chatting with Red Fang and June. They're both angry and demanding the Ether device so they can travel to the future.

Red Fang yells, "Why should we sit back and die?"

Out of nowhere, someone grabs me from behind. "Don't move, or else," a voice says.

I know that voice; it's the woman from the train. What is she doing here? How did she find us?

Ollie turns and sees me being held captive, then looks back at Red Fang, who now holds up a tomahawk. I don't know what to do, so I say a prayer. I ask God to help Ollie and me out of this situation.

Soon after, my purse begins to shake violently, and out of nowhere, I hear a warm sound. I turn around and see a cast-iron frying pan held above the lady's head—she releases me. The frying pan then drops, landing on her left foot, and she starts jumping and screaming.

I run over to Ollie, my mind racing as I wonder who—or what—hit the woman with the frying pan. Just as I reach him, she gets back up, brushing herself off. Now everyone is staring at her.

She pulls an Ether device from her pocket and points it at us.

"The coordinates are set to the middle of nowhere—2280," she sneers.

Then a voice corrects her.

"That's not true," Ollie says calmly. "It's the middle of a Rebel camp. And we all know how much the Rebels love us city folk."

The woman throws her head back and cackles, completely unhinged.

Suddenly, the frying pan swings again, this time hitting the Ether device squarely. I spot a young lady—about Octavius's size—in a floral prairie dress, her hair tied back in a neat bun.

"Run!" she yells, her voice strong and urgent.

The woman recovers quickly, grinning wildly. "It doesn't matter how far you run or how far apart you get," she says. "I can adjust the portal beam to fit something as big as a hot air balloon."

At that, Red Fang's ears perk up.

She raises the Ether device again, pointing the beam at us. But the little hologram leaps at her face and yanks off a mask, revealing something none of us expected.

Everyone gasps—it's none other than Matilda. She looks both embarrassed and determined. She throws the mask at the hologram, then tries to stomp it as it scurries away.

Matilda turns around, clearly annoyed, and shouts, "Now let's try that again, shall we?"

Ollie and I take off running as she makes the portal beam expand and shrink, laughing hysterically at our escape attempt. Meanwhile, Red Fang has been silently watching. She places her hands on the device and creeps behind the lady, quietly picking the frying pan up off the ground.

Red Fang tries to hit her over the head, but the lady spins around and screams, "Not you too!" She starts to point the portal beam at him, but he dashes in front of his tribe, about four hundred people. Matilda yells that she can make all of them fit into the portal, trying to stop her. She doesn't realize Red Fang isn't on our side at all.

Matilda points the portal beam at the tribe and activates it. Ollie and I run to the right side of the beam, then duck behind the cabin while she holds her aim. My purse starts shaking violently, and suddenly Octavius jumps out. I yell for him to come back, but he doesn't, so Ollie and I run back to the front of the cabin. Matilda stands in front of the portal, and the tribe is gone.

She looks at us and says, "Now, it's your turn."

Matilda starts laughing hysterically again as she presses buttons on her Ether device. But before she can act—standing there, confident—Octavius suddenly flies at her with a frying pan and strikes her in the stomach. She immediately falls back, dropping the Ether device. Octavius picks it up, presses Enter, and leaps back away from the portal.

A bright light flashes, blinding us for a few seconds. I smell that same strong, stale air from the day I first saw Damien. Octavius chuckles and tells us what we missed at the Rebels camp. Imagine a portal opening, and suddenly an entire Native American tribe—and Matilda—come through. He bets she and Red Fang have a few words for each other.

I feel both relieved and fearful about what comes next. Just then, the ranchers casually walk up to the bunkhouse, utterly unaware of what just happened.

I quickly grab the Ether device and examine it. Octavius hides behind Ollie's left leg, keeping out of sight. The screen displays two locations that have been programmed. I show it to Ollie.

"This might come in handy," he says. "We'll probably need to find the tribe and bring them back."

I look down, the weight of it hitting me again. Just by being here, I've disrupted the time continuum in a significant way. Ollie glances at me.

"We have to try to fix it," he says gently.

I nod. "You're right."

He hesitates for a moment. "There's something else I want to tell you."

I brace myself. "Okay."

"I held back earlier. At the dinner table." He looks down, then back at me. "I do have a dream. I want to be a pastor. I didn't know what you'd think of that."

I smile slightly, touched he's finally shared it. We both fall quiet, thinking about everything ahead—this mess we've made of the time continuum, and how to start putting it back together.

CHAPTER 8

Ollie and I stand there, looking at each other for a few minutes, unsure of what to do. I break the silence by suggesting we go back to Vicki's tonight. Ollie says it would be inappropriate for him to stay at the orphanage, and with nightfall approaching, he suggests we stay here for the night and head back first thing in the morning.

I suggest to Ollie that we ask Raquel to discuss bringing her tribe back with June. June might be open to her. I don't think June—or the Yellow Falcon tribe—cares much about our views on the disruption to the time continuum.

Ollie agrees and says it's probably our best bet, though he doesn't expect much to come of it. We'll likely need to find an alternative way to fix the time continuum issue. I understand how the tribe feels; it's a tragic situation.

Meanwhile, Oscar and Octavius are still examining the new hologram. After Ollie and I settle on a rough draft of a plan, I look down at her and ask Octavius if he knew she was there. He says he tried to get my attention, but the woman bumped into me. She had dropped the hologram device into my purse because each device can be tracked.

I start to feel foolish, realizing how distracted I've been by Ollie. I didn't notice any of this happening around me.

Octavius looks up at me. "Don't feel too bad," he says. "It's not every day you meet someone you really like."

I glance at Ollie and catch him smiling. I blush a little.

Octavius continues, "Next time your purse goes crazy, maybe check on me first. I usually have a good reason."

I nod. "You're right. I'll be more attentive."

With that settled, we all turn our focus back to the new hologram. I take a breath and ask, "What's your name?"

"My name is Ava," she replies.

"That's a beautiful name," I tell her.

Ava smiles and seems curious about Oscar, watching him with interest. I turn to her.

"Have you ever had a student you taught?" I ask.

She looks down. "Matilda."

Her voice is soft, and she begins to explain. "Ever since we were young, she was cruel to me—throwing me around, stomping on me."

I pause, then say gently, "Would you like to come with us? I don't feel right leaving you out here—to lose charge and eventually be forgotten."

Ava's face lights up. "Yes, please."

Octavius cuts in, cautious. "Matilda can trace her location."

"I know," I say. "But it's okay for now. Once we're back in our time, we'll drop Ava off at the education department. They can recycle her and assign her a new student."

Ava jumps for joy, thrilled by the plan, though I notice Octavius still looks uneasy.

I turn to him. "Her dislike for Matilda seems real. I don't think she's pretending to gain our trust. She wants to get away from her. And we happen to be the ones helping her do it."

He doesn't argue, but his expression stays wary.

The sky is darkening now, and sleepiness is settling in.

"I'll take Ava to the bunkhouse," Ollie says. "Just in case someone shows up during the night."

I nod. "I'll stay here in the cabin with Oscar and Octavius."

"I've got the shotgun with me in the bunkhouse," he adds. "If anyone comes, I'm better prepared for it."

Ollie leads Ava to the bunkhouse, reminding her to stay quiet so the ranchers don't hear. I watch them leave for a moment, then head into the cabin. I leave Oscar and Octavius downstairs and go up to the loft to sleep. I can hear them running around from time to time, but I'm too tired to get up, even if I want the noise to stop. Eventually, I drift off.

I have a dream. I'm standing on a cliff, looking down at a shallow pool of clear water—like a plunge pool. It's so shallow that I know it wouldn't even reach my knees. Off to the right, there's a canoe I want to get into. I start down a natural trail that winds along the cliff's edge and leads toward the water.

As I approach and wade in, the water deepens. Before long, it reaches my waist. The plunge pool is gone, replaced by a murky river tinged white and green, with a growing current. I spot the canoe again to my right, but I feel a vine wrapped around me, pulling to the left—drawing me away from the canoe and into the stronger, faster-moving river.

I wake up feeling unsettled, remembering the way the water suddenly rose and how eerie the murky current looked. I want to get up and grab a drink, but the cabin is still and quiet now. I don't want to wake Oscar, so I decide to stay in bed and try to fall back asleep. I lay there for a while before finally drifting off.

I have another lucid dream. This time, I'm back at the same cliff. As I stand near the edge, I suddenly begin to slip. I can't stop myself. I fall, but instead of waking up, I hit the ground. I find myself in a dark, unbearably hot place. When I look up, I see a white staircase with a person on each step. Some faces are familiar, others are not. I see Vicki and Ollie among them, both looking down at me.

I freeze for a moment, then a giant hand reaches down and begins to lift me toward the staircase, guiding me to the only empty spot. But as I rise, I feel something else—another set of hands grabbing me from behind, trying to pull me back. I can't see them, but I know they're long, with sharp fingernails. The hands are scorching hot, and a strong smell of sulfur fills the air.

I glance back at the staircase and see everyone reaching for me, trying to pull me up. Ollie is crying. I keep slipping backward, down toward the hidden figure behind me.

Then a blinding light appears, and suddenly I'm in a grassy field. It's quiet, and the only thing there is a small lamb up ahead. I begin walking toward it. The lamb sees me and comes closer, looking at me for a moment. I hear footsteps behind me and feel something—large, black, and evil—approaching. I don't turn around. I keep my eyes on the lamb.

The presence moves closer. I glance behind me briefly, then quickly look back at the lamb, planning to move toward it. But when I turn fully, I stop in my tracks—the lamb is now covered in blood. It steps closer and says, "Get under my blood. It's the only place you're safe from the enemy."

"Who is this enemy?" I ask.

"The one behind you," the lamb replies. "The one who comes to kill, steal, and destroy whoever he finds. He saw you while roaming the earth. He wants to destroy you, just like everyone not on the staircase."

"Why doesn't he destroy the people on the staircase, too?"

The lamb looks up at me. "Because they are under the blood. Once on the staircase, it becomes a place the enemy cannot go. Only those under my blood can enter."

I wake up and lie still, processing the dream. Through the window, I see the sun rising. I decide to get up and make tea. The dreams linger, leaving me uneasy. I think about Ollie and how he appeared on the staircase. I don't fully understand the meaning yet, but I know I will in time.

After making tea, I sit quietly with Oscar as the morning light grows. Then I hear a knock on the door.

"It's me," a familiar voice calls.

I open the door to find Ollie standing there with a plate of eggs, bacon, biscuits, and gravy. He says the ranchers cooked and had extra, so they let us have some. I take the plate and offer him tea, since I've just made it. It works out perfectly.

Ollie accepts the tea and heads back to get his plate. When he returns, we sit and eat together. I still feel tired, knowing I didn't get much restful sleep. Ollie tells me the ranchers will head out soon, and once they're gone, we can use the Ether device to return to Vicki.

"Why do you want to use it, considering all the problems it's caused?" I ask.

"It'll get us to Vicki much faster," he says. "She's always there first thing in the morning. It's important to talk to her before Raquel. We need Vicki on our side—Raquel will listen to her, even if reluctantly."

I nod, understanding. "Okay. But I want to stop using the device after this. It causes too many issues."

He agrees, and we finish breakfast.

Afterward, we gather our things, including Octavius and Ava, whom I carefully place in my purse along with everything else. We repack everything into the luggage bag. I hold out the Ether device, now programmed with the orphanage's coordinates. The ranchers have already left, and no one is around.

I activate the device. It pulses in my hand. I adjust the beam slightly so we all fit comfortably, and just like that, we step through the portal and arrive in front of the orphanage.

We pick ourselves up off the ground, head toward the orphanage, and look for Vicki. I knock on the front door. After a short wait, Philip answers. He sees me and immediately calls for Vicki. She comes to the door, looking concerned.

"What happened?" she asks.

I explained everything that happened yesterday. Vicki listens carefully, then invites us inside and makes us tea.

As we sit down, she says, "I want to help. We need to come up with a plan to restore the time continuum."

I look at her, pausing for a moment. Then I ask, plainly, "Do you really want to go back?"

"Why did you trust me right away?"

She doesn't seem surprised by the question. "I prayed a lot to God after overhearing the conversation between Ms. Collins and Matilda—about the Others," she explains. "God told me that a woman matching your description would eventually come through the portal the Others kept talking about. He said I would be the instrument of your miracle, as well as Raquel's. He told me to help you with lodging and food. The rest, He said, would be provided by someone else."

Vicki smiles softly. "I was relieved when Ollie stepped up to help. I don't have much to give with the orphanage running on what little we have." She pauses, then adds, "I pray without ceasing for Raquel. And just recently, God answered me. He said it will be all right with her soon."

I hesitate, but then ask, "Why is Raquel so different from you?" I know it's a personal question, probably offensive, but I feel compelled to understand.

Vicki looks at me with quiet understanding. "When we were kids, our dad left us. No warning, no explanation. He just left and never came back. That lack of a good father figure broke something in Raquel."

"Why didn't it affect you the same way?"

"Oh, it did," she says gently. "But later, I met a traveling evangelist who introduced me to Christ. That's when things began to shift. I stopped identifying as the abandoned daughter of Jack Higgins and started seeing myself as the daughter of God. Raquel, though, still sees herself as Jack Higgins's daughter, the one who was left behind and forgotten."

Vicki stands and offers us pastries or anything else we might want. I glance at Ollie, who shakes his head and thanks her for the tea.

Oscar is on the floor next to me, calmly licking his paws after his milk. We get up to go, and I can tell Vicki has a full day ahead. Still, I realize we haven't made much of a plan yet.

As we're leaving, Vicki tells me, "We'll see how it goes with Raquel. If things don't go well, I'll step in and help find a solution." She explains that she's hopeful and believes God will make a way, regardless, because all things work together for those who love the Lord.

"Do you think Raquel loves God?" I ask.

It's another question that feels a bit too blunt, maybe even offensive. But Vicki answers without hesitation. "If she did, she'd be obedient. But she's not right now. She's living in sin and prioritizing the world over God. Still," she adds, "I have faith God will intervene and lead her to salvation."

We head out to find Raquel, deciding to start at her workplace. As we near the alley, I glance around for Damien and his associates. I don't see anyone, so I keep walking—but I stay alert, especially watching out for Matilda.

We arrive and step inside. It takes a moment for my eyes to adjust from the bright sunlight to the dim interior of the bar. After a few seconds, I spot Raquel at the back, cleaning the counter, clearing up what looks like the remnants of the night before, getting ready for the next shift.

Ollie and I walk toward her. At first, she doesn't notice us, lost in her thoughts, her face tense with worry. As we get closer, a few floorboards creak beneath our feet. She looks up. I can tell she's been crying; she quickly wipes her eyes when she sees us. The sight makes me hesitate, and I take a small step back.

Ollie steps forward. "Have you heard anything about June lately?" he asks.

Raquel looks confused. "Why? Has something happened to her?" Her voice rises slightly. "Is it the government? Are they finally trying to remove her tribe from the reservation?"

In that moment, I realize Vicki never told me whether Raquel knows about the Others or the time portals.

I speak gently. "June's gone to Illinois."

Raquel blinks, puzzled. "Did the government send them? To a reservation in Illinois?"

I look at Raquel and say, "Not exactly. She left on her own, and her tribe went with her."

Now, Raquel looks even more confused. Ollie steps in.

"June's in Illinois," he says, "but it's not 1880. It's the year 2280."

Raquel stares at us, stunned, disbelief written across her face. Ollie continues, "We need your help to bring June and her tribe back to 1880."

Still in shock, Raquel shakes her head. "What do you think I can do about that?"

"You can talk to her," I explain. "Help convince her and the tribe to return. If they stay in 2280, the time continuum won't be restored."

Raquel looks down, then back at us. "I'll think about it," she says quietly.

I try to press a little more. "Please, just come talk to her."

But she cuts me off. "I can't even help myself. Why would you think I can help with the time continuum?"

Just then, Frank walks in and crosses his arms. The message is clear. It's time for us to go and try again later. I ask Raquel, "Will you be at church tomorrow evening?"

She replies, "If the Lord's willing for me to be."

Frank nods. "Ain't that the truth?"

We leave and head back to the orphanage, hoping to find Vicki. She's busy helping a customer place an order for curtains. Once the customer leaves, we explain everything that happened with Raquel.

Vicki asks me to stay the night and offers Ollie the now-empty room that used to belong to Ms. Collins and Matilda.

She insists we speak to Raquel again after church tomorrow evening. "Giving her a little time to think things through has always helped," she says. "It gives her space to decide for herself."

I agree, though I hesitate, thinking about Frank showing up. I hope he doesn't try to stop her from coming tomorrow.

CHAPTER 9

The next day, Ollie and I get up early to look for Raquel. We don't expect to talk to her until church this evening, but we want to see what's going on with Frank and how much trouble she might be in because of him.

Ollie suggests we have brunch at the Corner Café. It's a good excuse to be in town in case Frank is around, and we can also stop by the general store. The walk into town and back will help pass the time while we wait for church.

We leave Oscar at the orphanage and take Octavius and Ava with us in my purse. I think to myself, *I'll look for a parasol in town today.* At least it could help block the sun. The walk is sunny and hot, but I keep sneaking glances at Ollie as he walks beside me, talking about the history of the area. He points out an old abandoned stagecoach and an empty cattle corral, sharing little bits of local lore.

He tells me the story of an outlaw who used to ride the trains around here years ago. "He was never caught, at least not around here," Ollie says. "No one ever heard what happened to him after he left, about ten years back."

"What was his name?" I ask.

"Falcon Eye. Better than a rake with a pistol."

I pause for a moment, considering the name. *What if Falcon Eye is a nickname for Jack Higgins?* I start to wonder when exactly he left his family.

We arrive at the Corner Café and enjoy a lovely brunch. By the time we sit down, it's already edging into lunchtime. I choose a seat by the window and quietly wish the place had air conditioning. I glance at Ollie as he studies the menu. I'm craving pork and beans with a cold glass of lemonade.

I begin to drift into thought and realize I'm thinking less and less about getting back home. The idea scares me. What if I really do get stuck here in 1880? Still, a part of me feels like this is where I'm supposed to be for now. But if the time continuum isn't fixed soon, what will the future even look like? Not just for me, but for everyone?

The waitress comes by, and I place my order. Ollie orders coffee, a pork chop, and potatoes. A short time later, our food arrives, and we eat slowly, enjoying the conversation about what life might be like when we get to California.

"I don't care what happens next," I say, smiling. "This moment is good."

"It is," Ollie agrees. "Feels kind of normal."

We finished brunch and paid, then decided to visit the general store. On the way, I spot Raquel standing in front of the train station. I wonder if she's waiting for someone or planning to leave.

"Should we go talk to her?" I ask.

Ollie glances over and shakes his head. "Let's leave her be for now. We can't force her to help. She'll come around if she's meant to."

I nod, even though part of me still thinks it might be better to ask what she's doing.

Inside the general store, I finally get a chance to browse. There are canned and dry goods stacked in barrels, but I'm most drawn to the kitchen items. The cookbooks and aprons make me smile. Ollie finds a small selection of parasols, and I choose a light blue one with a white handle. He pays for it, and we leave the store.

We continue through town, window shopping, when I spot Frank speaking with a young woman. He hasn't seen us. The way he stands so close to her, it's obvious she's more than a friend.

I tilt my parasol slightly to hide my face and walk a bit closer, trying to hear what they're saying.

"I told you, I'll get the money as soon as Raquel pays those gambling debts," Frank says.

The woman crosses her arms. "You said that last week."

"My friends are doing great pretending to be swindled gamblers. She's falling for it completely," Frank says, laughing.

They both grin cruelly.

"She really thinks you love her," the woman says.

"What a fool," Frank replies. "She has no idea we're about to take everything she has."

I take a step back, thinking to myself how strange it is. That woman isn't even beautiful, and yet Frank is plotting to defraud a woman like Raquel—someone truly gorgeous, not just in looks but in heart. She's been willing to risk everything to save him from supposed men who would hurt him over gambling debts.

And to think that this woman is part of Frank's plan, knowing full well where the money is coming from. Their relationship appears to be founded on the thrill of inflicting pain on others. I can't comprehend that kind of deceit, that level of manipulation.

I turn to look at Ollie. His expression is one of genuine shock, as if he had no idea about Frank's plan. Before we leave, I hear the woman say, "We need the money by tonight if we're going to leave tomorrow morning."

I freeze. That means after church, they'll come to collect the money from Raquel.

As we walk away, I hold the parasol behind us to block their view. It's a good thing I do, because I hear the woman ask, "Do you think they heard us?"

Frank replies casually, "It doesn't matter. We're leaving tomorrow morning anyway. Raquel's convinced I love her and that we're getting married soon."

I quicken my pace, and Ollie keeps up as we make our way back to the orphanage. I have no idea how I'm going to break this to Vicki. I know it's going to devastate her. The thought of tonight is starting to make me nervous.

"Would you like to pray about this with me?" Ollie asks gently.

I hesitate. "Maybe we should wait until we're back at the orphanage.

Somewhere private. I don't want anyone overhearing us and running off to warn Frank or his friends."

Ollie nods. "Good idea."

We walk quickly, and once we're back at the orphanage, Vicki greets us and offers tea. Without thinking, I blurt out, "I need something stronger than tea."

Vicki looks at me with concern. "What happened?"

I tell her everything: what we overheard between Frank and the woman by the train station.

Vicki listens, stunned. "I have no idea who she could be. Frank keeps his personal life so private. He won't even answer basic questions without getting defensive."

We sit together in the living room. Vicki looks down, a look of sadness on her face. "I knew something was off about him. But Raquel kept saying he had a rough childhood. She used it to excuse how closed off he is."

She sighs deeply. "Now she's in danger. If she doesn't give him the money, I know what people like Frank are capable of. And if she does, she'll lose everything."

Her voice softens. "And the worst part is, she still believes these people are her friends."

Ollie suggests we pray for Raquel. He and Vicki take turns, each offering a heartfelt prayer on her behalf. I feel awkward and uncomfortable, but I add a short prayer of protection for her. When we finish, Vicki heads to the kitchen to prepare some tea.

As we wait, I notice Ollie pacing in the living room. He looks deep in thought. I have a feeling he's thinking about something he wants to add to the plan for tonight—something I won't like. But for now, he's keeping it to himself.

Vicki returns with tea and a small tray of pastries.

"These are just a little thank-you," she says, setting them down. "For looking out for Raquel and telling me the truth about Frank."

I can tell Raquel hasn't had many people truly invested in her. That's probably why she ended up with Frank—because he acted like he cared.

We have dinner at Vicki's while the children and Pricilla are outside tending to the garden and finishing chores. After dinner, we all went our separate ways for a while. Ollie and Vicki leave the living room, and I stay behind, watching Oscar sleep. He's curled up with his ball of yarn, softly snoring, and I can't help but smile at how peaceful and adorable he looks.

As we prepare to go to church, Ollie suggests I bring Oscar along in case we need to use the Ether device.

"It's better to be safe," he says.

He's probably right, though I hope we won't need it. I gently pick up the sleeping Oscar and place him in a picnic basket that Vicki lent me. That way, he can rest and still be nearby if we need to activate the portal.

The three of us head out to church. The walk feels long and heavy, filled with quiet anxiety and uncertainty. Ollie walks between Vicki and me as I carry Oscar in the picnic basket along with my purse. He offers to take Oscar.

"You can carry him on the way back," I say, hoping the small joke lightens the mood a bit.

We finally reach the church and see Raquel ahead of us, stepping inside.

"At least she's here," I whisper. "We can keep her safe from Frank and his gang tonight."

Inside, I scan the room and spot Raquel sitting alone near the front. It makes sense—June isn't here.

The three of us sit in the back row, planning to speak with Raquel after the sermon. The church is full, and the service has begun. Music from the piano fills the space as the congregation stands and sings hymns. I read along in the hymn book. Vicki and Ollie sing as well, their voices blending with the others. For a brief moment, the mood feels lighter.

The sermon gets underway as we take our seats, and the preacher begins to speak. I keep my eyes on Raquel, watching as she dabs her eyes with a handkerchief. She appears to be crying. I glance over at Vicki, who is listening intently to the message. The picnic basket shifts a bit as Oscar, now awake, squirms in protest at being confined.

My attention sharpens when the preacher reads from John 1:51.

"And he saith unto him, Verily, verily, I say unto you, Hereafter ye shall see heaven open, and the angels of God ascending and descending upon the Son of man."

The preacher explains this as a vision of a staircase between heaven and earth. The image jolts me—I remember my dream. I glance around the church and notice familiar faces. People who were in the dream. Vicki. Ollie. My heart starts to race as I turn my focus from Raquel to the sermon.

The preacher continues, reading from Romans 5:9.

"Since, therefore, we have now been justified by his blood, much more shall we be saved by him from the wrath of God."

Then he turns to Ephesians 1:7.

"In him, we have redemption through his blood, the forgiveness of our trespasses, according to the riches of his grace."

My heart pounds as I recall the lamb in my dream, covered in blood, telling me that only under his blood would I be safe from the dark presence behind me.

Everything around me begins to blur. For a few moments, all I can hear is my heartbeat. As I settle down, I realize the sermon has ended.

The preacher invites anyone who wants to accept Jesus Christ into their heart to come forward and repeat a prayer.

"Dear Lord Jesus, I know that I am a sinner, and I ask for Your forgiveness. I believe You died for my sins and rose from the dead. I turn from my sins and invite You to come into my heart and life."

Sitting quietly, I whisper the words.

Ollie, seated between us, turns to look at me. His eyes are wide. He heard me say the prayer. He knows I accepted Jesus into my life.

The service ends, and people begin to rise. Vicki jumps up, clearly eager to speak with Raquel. As Raquel approaches, Vicki turns to her.

"Can we speak to you in private?" she asks

"Alright, but it has to be fast," Raquel says. "I have a train to catch."

"Where are you going?" Vicki asks.

"As far away from here as I can afford to go," Raquel replies.

I understand what she means. Instead of giving Frank the money he's been demanding for his fake gambling debts, she used it to buy herself a one-way ticket out of town.

Ollie speaks up. "Let's take this outside and talk."

We all agree. I pick up the picnic basket and my purse, and we step out to the front of the church. But before we can say a word to Raquel, two of Frank's friends appear. They had clearly been waiting for her to come out.

They charge toward us, yelling.

"You'd better pay what Frank owes, or you're dead!"

I stare at them, stunned. I can't believe they're taking this scam so far that they'd threaten her life over a fake debt.

Before I can react, Vicki and Ollie both draw their revolvers. The situation escalates in an instant. The two men pull out their guns and fire at us. Ollie shouts.

"Run! Zig-zag to the nearest building!"

He returns fire as we sprint. My heart pounds. I quickly check the picnic basket to make sure Oscar is safe, and I notice my purse shaking, pulling at my shoulder.

Just as Vicki and I turn to run, Ollie yells out.

"I love you!"

His words stop me for a second. I look back at him. He's facing the men, firing. Then, out of nowhere, more gunfire rings out from the west.

We all turn, and to my horror, it's Damien and Windell.

I shout, "Don't you have anything better to do than follow us around?"

Damien laughs. "No, I don't."

He and Windell walk toward us. Raquel stares at Damien in disbelief. Frank's two friends pause, uncertain now. Their faces show a mix of shock and fear as they listen.

Damien steps closer.

"Aw, isn't this sweet? Trying to save each other."

"Stay back or else!" I yell.

Damien smiles with a smug grin as he stops approaching. He isn't taking this seriously at all. He thinks he has the upper hand.

"What are you going to do to me?" he asks.

I hesitate for a second, then act on impulse. I throw the picnic basket at him. It hits him squarely, and out comes Oscar, who lets out the most horrifying growl and begins clawing at Damien wildly.

As this unfolds, Frank's two friends try to run. But instead of fleeing to the side or back toward the church, they bolt forward, straight toward Raquel.

Damien struggles to get Oscar off of him. He finally succeeds and immediately reaches for his Ether device. But with fresh claw marks and in a state of shock, he fumbles. He doesn't notice where Oscar is pointing. A portal activates right in front of the two men. They scream as they're pulled in and vanish.

I dig into my purse and grab one of the two Ether devices without checking which one it is. I activate it.

"Oscar!" I yell.

He sprints toward me, and I scoop him up. Raquel runs over just as I feel the Ether device begin to pulse. Time seems to pause for a heartbeat. Ollie moves in closer. Vicki backs away, instinctively understanding what I'm about to do. She's never seen a portal open this close before.

I hold Oscar tightly as Raquel and Ollie grab onto me. I look back at Vicki. She stands frozen, her face pale with shock. I reach out to her, but it's too late. The portal pulls us through.

The next thing I know, I'm on the ground in a vast, empty field. I don't want to move. I have no idea where we are. The only comfort is knowing we still have the coordinates to the orphanage on the other Ether device.

Then Raquel screams.

"What's wrong?" I ask, getting up quickly.

"We left Vicki," she says. "What if that monster hurts her?"

"She's probably okay," Ollie says. "They were after the Ether device, not Vicki."

Raquel starts to panic. "What just happened? Where are we? What is this Ether thing? Why does that man want it?"

I feel exhausted, drained by everything. We have no idea where we are, and we have no shelter, food, or water.

"I can answer your questions," I say.

Before I can continue, my purse begins to move and tug again. Raquel's eyes widen.

"What's wrong with it?" she asks, staring at the movement. "Why is it moving?"

Octavius climbs out and tips his hat.

"Howdy," he says, waving.

Raquel lets out a scream that echoes across the field and nearly faints.

CHAPTER 10

Octavius ducks back into my purse as Ollie gently tries to calm Raquel.

"Listen," Ollie says, "we overheard Frank talking to a woman. He's been using you. The plan was to get you to pay for their train tickets to New York by having two of his friends pretend Frank owed them gambling debts."

Raquel stares at him, silent.

"Those men who keep threatening you? They were part of the act. Frank and that woman are involved romantically. He's been pretending to be in love with you to get your money."

Ollie pauses.

"This was the conversation we were going to have with you at the church—before everything happened."

Raquel lowers her eyes as the truth sinks in.

"He did ask me how much savings I had," she says softly. "He even asked for small loans now and then, but he never paid them back."

She shakes her head.

"I feel so stupid. I should have seen this coming. I should've known better."

Her face changes as her thoughts turn to Vicki.

"I left her behind," she says, horrified. "What if something happens to her?"

"She's strong," I tell her. "She's a woman of faith. I know God will protect her."

I pause, scanning the wide field around us. Bright green grass stretches in every direction, speckled with colorful wildflowers. Blue Jays and Cardinals flit overhead. We're clearly no longer in Arizona, and certainly not in the desert.

I glance at the sky. Storm clouds are starting to gather in the distance. A growing unease settles over me. We're out here in the middle of nowhere, with no shelter, no food, and no idea where exactly we are.

Ollie watches the sky too. None of us speaks for a while.

Then Raquel breaks the silence.

"Was that really a talking squirrel?" she asks.

I glance at Ollie and nod.

"We're near the Rebels," I say. "Matilda used these coordinates for a reason. They match the ones the Yellow Falcon Tribe used to."

Raquel is quiet. I take a deep breath.

"We were going to ask you at the church if you'd help us talk to June," I say. "To see if she and her tribe would agree to return to Arizona in 1880. It's part of how we need to fix the time continuum."

Raquel gazes off into the distance, lost in thought.

"I can talk to June," she says quietly. "If we ever cross paths again in this lifetime. But she's probably long gone. Who knows where? Or when?"

I feel a light breeze as the scent of rain fills the air. The sky hasn't opened yet, but it's coming. I wonder what will happen next, knowing we're about to be drenched. Ollie turns to me.

"Should we use the other Ether device and go back to the orphanage?"

"It's not a bad idea," I say. "If nothing else happens soon, it might be our only option. We can't stay stranded out here."

Just then, a deep rumble rises—not from the sky, but from the ground.

I pick up Oscar as the sound grows louder. Ollie steps closer to me. Raquel listens carefully, then says, "I know that sound."

Before she can explain, a herd of wild horses crests the hill. Dozens of them, scattered and swift, charging straight toward us.

"Which way do we go?" I shout.

The thunder of hooves drowns out everything else. The horses are closing in fast. Then, cutting through the chaos, I hear a voice—familiar and commanding—calling out to someone among the herd.

From behind the herd, I spot June riding a horse, flanked by several members of her tribe. They're chasing the herd, guiding them toward a distant corral.

When June sees us, she pulls up and rides over, visibly surprised.

"Where have you been?" I ask quickly.

She gives me a puzzled look. "You know we went into the future."

"I know," I say. "But we've been looking for you."

June raises an eyebrow. "This is a strange time to look for someone. Why?"

"We need to fix the time continuum. You and your tribe have to come back."

Her face hardens.

"We're not going back," she says flatly. "We like it here. Life is better now. We've joined the Rebel group in this region. They support us living our way, peaceful and free.

I turn to Ollie and Raquel.

"I wasn't expecting this," I tell them quietly. "They're part of the Rebels now. And they're happy."

"But they have to go back," Raquel says. "They don't belong here."

I nod slowly. "It's not an option. The timeline has to be corrected."

I turn back, but June is already staring at me—her expression no longer calm, but sharp with fury.

"You expect us to go back to our deaths?" she screams.

The words hang in the air.

I almost say yes. But I stop myself. None of us speaks. We stare at each other. The riders and the rest of the herd have moved on, leaving us behind in the silence, alone with June.

Then we hear another sound—deep, slow, and heavy. A large animal crests the hill.

It's a bison.

I stare at it for a long moment, then murmur under my breath, "Ain't that something?"

June asks me what I meant by that. I explain that bison were hunted almost to extinction in the wild but managed to survive in smaller numbers in a few national parks and wildlife sanctuaries. After the nuclear war, the few that remained must have multiplied and started appearing plentiful in the wild again.

"How did the bison almost become extinct?" June asks.

I pause, knowing the truth: that settlers hunted them nearly out of existence. June looks at me, already knowing the answer.

She says quietly, "The bison and I are better off left alone in the future."

Thunder rumbles through the sky, loud and sharp. June looks up, then turns her eyes to the bison, which is beginning to show signs of aggression. Her tan horse rears slightly, sensing the tension as the bison edges closer.

June turns to us. "We need to go."

Raquel asks, "Where can we take shelter from the storm?"

"We can go back to the Rebels' camp," June says.

I tense up, and June notices, but she says nothing. She gestures for us to follow. We walk east for about fifteen minutes. Light sprinkles start to fall as buildings come into view ahead.

Matilda was right. She had planned to send us to the Rebels, and here we are—guided by the coordinates she gave us. I have no idea what to expect. Ollie glances at me with clear concern.

"Are the Rebels on good terms with people from your time?" he asks.

"Not really," I admit.

"Then why are we walking into a Rebel settlement just because it seems like the only option?" he says. "We have the other Ether device. We could activate it and avoid all of this. June already gave us her answer. She's not interested in helping restore the time continuum. Any options involving the Yellow Falcon Tribe seem off the table."

I don't know what to say. I feel helpless and deeply frustrated with how this is all unfolding. But I can only blame myself. I should have gone back as soon as I figured out how to use the Ether device. I know June and her tribe feel the same—that it's my fault. And I can't expect them to fix my mistake.

Ollie looks at me and says, "God will make a way through all of this. He'll bring it to His will."

"I hope so, Ollie," I reply. "Because short of throwing an entire tribe through the portal against their will, I don't know how to fix this."

As we get closer to the settlement, I am reminded of adobe-style buildings from out west. Large, multilevel structures with flat rooftops, some covered in grass and others with gardens full of fruit trees and raised vegetable beds.

Instead of wooden ladders, the buildings feature stairs, and the surrounding grounds are filled with orchards and additional gardens, clearly designed to feed a large group of people. I expected to see something more fortified, but the settlement is surprisingly open and colorful. Decorative tiles line the doors and stairs, and I imagine similar patterns cover the interior walls. A short distance away, there's a horse round pen and adobe barns, which surprises me—they've chosen adobe over wood here, too.

As we enter the settlement, people start to take notice of us. A crowd begins to gather, and I feel very uncomfortable. Ollie notices and turns to June.

"Is it necessary to have a crowd around us? If we're staying, is there a place we can sleep tonight?"

June nods. "There's a small home not in use right now. You can stay there."

She leads us to it, and I ask, "Where will you stay?"

"My tribe has built hogans farther east. We've made our own settlement there," she says.

As we walk, I hear whispers among the Rebels and try not to draw attention to myself. Dressed in 1880s clothing, I blend in reasonably well, but I'm still uneasy. I don't fully trust June to keep quiet about where I'm from, though I suspect she's keeping the peace for Raquel's sake.

We arrive at the first building in the settlement—a two-story structure with a rooftop garden. We open the door farthest to the right, which appears to be an apartment unit. Inside, a large room greets us, adorned with beautiful tiles on the walls and ceiling. A staircase to the left is also tiled.

In the center of the room are four soft, coral-colored couches arranged in a square. Between them sits a low, wide table. It's too low to be a coffee table, so I assume it's used for dining. The living room layout is compact, and it seems that most daily life happens outside.

Behind the couches is a small, modern kitchenette. To the right of the seating area is a contemporary fireplace, with a neat stack of wood beside it.

Under the stairs is a built-in bookcase with a few books and some knick-knacks. On my second scan of the house, I notice a thick, colorful area rug under the couches and table. Aside from the ceiling light, that's about it on the first floor—except for a door I hadn't noticed before, tucked behind the staircase. It's either a pantry or a half bathroom.

I glance at Ollie and Raquel. They look stunned. It's their first time seeing a modern-style home. I notice a washing machine tucked next to the dishwasher in the kitchenette, and I can tell they're curious about everything. I plan to go over it all with them later this evening.

Suddenly, June speaks, startling me. I'd forgotten she was still here. She says there's a little food in the kitchen that should last us through the night. I turn and thank her, though she looks at me with a stern expression.

Then she adds, almost as an afterthought, "There are three small bedrooms upstairs with a full bathroom. There's also a half bathroom just around the corner."

She tells us she'll come back tomorrow morning to check in and hear what plans we've made for returning to Rocky Creek. I feel a wave of annoyance at her. She seems utterly unconcerned about the state of the time continuum. Then she looks at Ollie.

"If you're still interested in being a preacher," she says, "there's an opening here. We don't have a church yet, but I've been wanting to start one for both the Rebels and the tribe."

I can tell Ollie is intrigued. Thunder rumbles again, and we realize the storm is nearly here. June excuses herself, saying she'll return in the morning.

I watch her leave, then ask, "Do you think June will make it to her house before the rain starts?"

Ollie shrugs. "I don't know. I'm more surprised she didn't want to stay here until the storm passed."

"Storms here aren't like in Arizona," I tell him. "They can last for hours, not just a quick downpour."

"That makes sense," Ollie replies. "Maybe it's better for her to try and get home now than wait all night."

I take the picnic basket and head upstairs to find a room to sleep in. Raquel follows, and we pick one out together. The bedrooms are narrow and simple, with folding mats on the floor for sleeping. Each room has a closet, built-in bookcases, and a small wicker cabinet for bedding and a few personal items.

Raquel stares at the bathroom, wide-eyed. She's never seen indoor plumbing before. I explain how everything works, and she seems amazed. Indoor plumbing did exist in the 1880s, but it was expensive and considered a luxury, so it's possible she's never encountered it until now.

As Raquel and I head back downstairs, we notice another staircase leading to the roof. We climb it and find a roof hatch at the top. I pull the latch, and it opens easily. We step onto the roof and see a beautiful garden. Some plants grow directly in the soil spread across the rooftop, while others are potted in colorful ceramic planters. Along the front wall sits a set of brown wicker patio furniture beneath a striped, multicolored canopy.

Suddenly, a loud crack of thunder splits the sky. Within seconds, rain pours down on us, soaking us completely. We dash back through the hatch and down the stairs into the house. I notice the staircase has traction strips on each step to prevent slipping on the tile.

Back in our rooms, Raquel and I change into dry clothes. I gather our wet clothes and show her how to use the washing machine. She loves it and says we're lucky to have such conveniences in the future. Meanwhile, Ollie opens the refrigerator and marvels at it.

"An electric icebox," he says, impressed.

I smile, amused by the term. He looks inside, but it's empty. I check the kitchen cabinets and find some canned vegetables and fruit, along with a box of tea and a tin of Danish butter cookies. I check the expiration dates—both are still good for about three more months. As I'm about to close the cabinet, I spot a few cans of cat food.

I grab one, find a plate, and set it down for Oscar. He happily digs in, clearly hungry. I prepare a tea kettle and get a plate ready for the cookies. Oscar rubs up against my legs as I move around the kitchen.

Then I notice my purse moving on the couch. Raquel watches it closely, clearly curious.

"Can I meet Octavius?" she asks.

I hesitate, then call for him to come out. He slowly emerges from the purse, but Ava suddenly rushes ahead of him. Raquel jumps back slightly.

"I thought you only had one computer," she says, surprised.

I explain Ava's situation and how she ended up with me. Raquel listens, then nods.

"Well," she says, "I don't know much about the future. I'd be willing to be Ava's student."

Ollie suggests we have a Bible study while we wait. I set the teacups and cookies on the table, and we snack as we read and discuss scripture together. It's peaceful. Eventually, the rain lets up, and there's a knock at the door.

I open it and find a few Rebel women standing outside, holding home-made dishes for us. One brought a casserole, the other a loaf of zucchini bread. I think they're asking if everything is okay in the house. I nod and tell them yes. They seem surprised we know how to use everything. After thanking them for the food, I shut the door a little too quickly, not wanting to stay and talk.

Ollie notices. "Why didn't you talk more with them?" he asks.

"They shouldn't find out I'm not really from the past," I explain. "I'm from one of the dome cities. That would raise too many questions."

Raquel and Ava are chatting and getting along well, while Octavius wanders the house, checking things out. In the early evening, we head to the rooftop. Under the canopy, surrounded by the garden, we enjoy the quiet. A few ripe persimmons hang from a tree nearby. Clear string lights are strung overhead, held by poles spaced along the edge. The rooftop balcony is beautiful, and I've made lemonade to go with the casserole for dinner.

As we eat, Ollie turns to me. "We need to start thinking of a plan. We're lucky to have this place for the night, maybe two at most."

"I agree," I say. "Tomorrow, we should try to talk with June one last time.

After that, we need to head toward the dome city where I'm from. I can use the reverse coordinates to get back to my house."

Raquel frowns. "How will that help if Louis is part of the Others?"

"He might not be," I say. "Louis is goofy and never takes things too seriously. That's not really the mindset the Others seem to have. It might not make him the best fit for museum work, but it also might mean he's not truly involved with them. At the very least, he might say something that gives us more insight into what the Others are working on. And if nothing else, we'll have a place to stay for a day or two before returning to the orphanage."

I pause for a moment, then add, "But we can't stay there long. The Others have already been to my house to kill me."

Ollie and Raquel stare at me in stunned silence. After that, no one says anything. We quietly finish our dinner.

CHAPTER 11

*A*fter dinner, we sit outside quietly, each of us lost in thought. No one speaks. None of us has a clear plan for tomorrow. We'll try to make our way to the Sanctuary, with the worst-case scenario being that we use the Ether device. I leave the zucchini bread in the refrigerator for breakfast, and Oscar has a can of cat food set aside for him as well.

Eventually, we head to bed. Ollie sleeps on the couch downstairs while Raquel and I each take a room. Oscar follows me and curls up beside me on the mat. As I try to fall asleep, I reflect on the silence of the night. We've faced more difficult situations before and still managed to talk. Maybe it's the awkwardness from Ollie's earlier confession. I never said I loved him back. Maybe he's hurt or unsure of what to say now. Raquel is probably quiet because she knows she has to have a difficult conversation with June in the morning.

I pray and ask God to guide us and let His will be done as we try to reach the Sanctuary.

Eventually, I drift off to sleep. In my dream, I'm being chased by a group of people with guns. I can't see their faces. I'm running for my life and almost get caught and shot. When I wake up, I see a large black figure on the wall in front of me. At first, I think it's Oscar, but then I realize cats can't climb walls, and this thing doesn't have a tail. I stare at it for a while until it simply disappears.

I fall back asleep. The next morning, I woke to the sound of Raquel knocking on the door.

"June's here," she says. "She wants to talk to us."

I wonder if it could really be this easy after I prayed. I get up, get dressed, and head downstairs. June is sitting on the couch, eating a slice of zucchini bread with a glass of milk. She must have poured it from what she brought for us.

Raquel, in good spirits, asks, "Do you want some zucchini bread too?" She cuts a slice and brings it to me with a glass of milk.

June doesn't seem worried or upset. She seems calm, and I can tell she hasn't changed her mind about staying. She eventually shifts her focus to me just as Ollie comes in from the roof carrying more persimmons.

June looks at me. "I can take you near the dome city, but we'll have to ride motorcycles."

"Wouldn't that attract a lot of attention?" I ask. "Why not use horses?"

"It's farther than you think," she says. "We use motorcycles when traveling to the ruins or going around the dome city. It's faster and more practical for the terrain."

I ask June if she'll reconsider having the tribe return to 1880. She shakes her head and looks down.

I let it go for now as we finish breakfast. Once Oscar has been fed, we gather our luggage. June escorts us out of the apartment and leads us toward a few spare motorcycles. On the way, some of the Rebels smile and try to strike up conversations. A rather large crowd begins to form, asking us questions about life in the past. I find it difficult to answer most of them.

Some in the crowd seem to notice my hesitation and begin directing their questions specifically at me. I try to shift attention away from myself and focus on reaching the motorcycles.

Once there, I realize we need a way to carry Oscar's picnic basket and our luggage. June shows me a small luggage rack on the back of the motorcycle and hands me a bungee cord to secure the basket. The luggage gets tied to the rack on the second motorcycle. I'm relieved it's working out so far.

As I start to climb onto the bike, someone from the crowd steps forward and tries to help by reaching for my purse.

"It's alright, I've got it," I say.

But the individual grabs it anyway, trying to pull it off my shoulder. I hold on, and soon we're in a brief tug of war. The purse hits the ground, and Octavius and Ava tumble out.

The crowd gasps.

One woman points and says, "Those are the things the domed city people take with them."

Shouts rise from the group, calling us traitors. I step forward.

"I'm the only one from the dome city. Ollie and Raquel have nothing to do with any of it."

June raises her voice. "Enough! Let them go. They're trying to stop the Others from carrying out their plan for world domination."

Her words catch me off guard. I didn't expect her to know that. Yes, she saw Matilda and the Ether device, but she shouldn't say that Matilda is one of the Others, or what they're planning.

The crowd inches closer. I turn to Ollie and Raquel.

"It's time to go," I say as Octavius and Ava leap back into my purse.

Ollie nods and jumps on a motorcycle. I climb onto the back behind him. June mounts the other bike, and Raquel climbs on behind her. We take off down a dirt path through the tall grass, heading toward the road.

June veers to the right, and we continue riding at high speed. I stay alert, aware that there's a chance we're being followed. We ride for a while until we draw near the ruins. June comes to a stop and stares ahead, her eyes fixed on the distant skyline. The skyscrapers are crumbling, slowly being overtaken by thick, creeping vegetation.

She cuts off the motorcycle and says, "Why can't people just get along? Why are we doomed to repeat the same mistakes as a species?"

Raquel speaks up. "Can I take a closer look at the ruins? I've never even seen a futuristic city—only the ruins of one."

Ollie looks toward the skyline. "What city is that?"

"Chicago," I tell him. "It was one of the biggest cities in America before the nuclear war."

He stands there quietly, taking in the decaying skyline in awe.

We agree to get a little closer, though not all the way into the city like the tour buses used to go. As we move forward, Ollie and Raquel ask a stream of questions about life in a modern city. I answer as best I can, though most of what I know comes from life inside the dome.

After a while, we stop to take a break. I can tell we're getting close to the Sanctuary, but I wish we had bottled water—or anything to drink, really. As we rest, I notice the picnic basket shifting around more than usual. I open the lid and take a peek inside. Oscar suddenly jumps out, startling me, and runs off a short distance.

"Oscar, come back!" I call, chasing after him.

As I start to run, I hear the rumble of approaching motorcycles. My heart races. It can only mean more Rebels. I'm unsure whether they're following up on June's settlement or if they're from a different group.

I yell even louder for Oscar. "Come back, now!"

Octavius calls from inside my purse. I let him out, and he immediately runs after Oscar. Ava vanishes without a word. Everything feels like it's spiraling out of control.

The sound of the motorcycles grows louder, and soon I can hear the engines coming from ahead of us. In the distance, I see them—at least a dozen riders closing in fast.

I look frantically for Oscar and Octavius in front of me, and for Ava, who has vanished somewhere behind me. The riders approach, slow down, and come to a halt in a line just ahead of us. Their masks are intimidating—skull designs paired with black feathers. The engines cut off, and I know they're about to speak.

Raquel stands behind me. Ollie is to my right. June stands confidently in front of me, facing the Rebels without flinching. I don't know how this will go until the first rider speaks. The voice is too familiar. I know immediately —it's Red Fang.

"What do you want?" I call out to him.

He turns to the Rebels and says, "She's the one who wants the tribe to return to a home where they all die."

A Rebel I've never seen before steps forward. "Of course, the domed people would think like that," he says. "You're the ones responsible for the nuclear war."

"That's not true," I say. "Why do you think we caused it?"

"You had the technology to make the weapons," the Rebel replies. "That makes you accountable."

"We all lived in the same world before the war," I tell him. "We were part of the same economy, using the same technologies. It wasn't the tech that caused it; it was poor leadership and bad decisions. A few powerful people made those choices, not everyone. And after the war, people did what they had to just to survive."

The Rebels fall silent for a few moments. Then Oscar suddenly appears, and Octavius is riding on his back. The sight of Octavius seems to trigger something in the Rebels. They begin to shift, posturing more aggressively.

"Why do you use things like that?" one of them asks, eyes narrowed at Octavius.

Oscar leaps back into the picnic basket, and Octavius jumps into my purse. Ava is still missing. I look around. We have a few options. I know using the Ether device might be the only way out.

"Why do you chase people from the dome cities when we come to see the ruins?" I ask.

"You're the reason for the calamity," one answers. "You shouldn't be here to cause it again."

"I don't buy that," I say. "It's too unrealistic."

Another Rebel steps forward. "Years ago, some strangers came around, and a large group of our Rebels disappeared. We don't know what happened to them. Maybe it hasn't happened to other groups, but it happened to ours."

I ask him what he means. He explains that, according to legend, a group of strange people once appeared, covered from head to toe in clothing and makeup. They didn't speak much and kept to themselves. Then, one morning, two hundred members of the community were just gone without a trace.

I begin to understand. This must be where the Others got the human DNA they needed to cross with. It explains why the Rebels are hostile toward Dome City people—they think we're the ones who did it. They don't know the truth about the Others, and they assume it was people from the dome cities in disguise. It's all starting to make sense now.

I step forward. "We have a common enemy," I say. "They're called the Others. They survived the nuclear war, but they were closer to the blasts and their DNA mutated. They're not peaceful. They want to go back to the past to regain power."

The Rebels begin murmuring among themselves. June walks over and joins their discussion.

Suddenly, I smell a strong, stale odor in the air. A wave of dread passes over me. I look around quickly, trying to spot anything out of place. I grab the picnic basket and call out for Ava. My voice draws everyone's attention, just as I hear footsteps approaching from behind.

I turn and there they are. Damien and Wendell. They're dressed in cowboy outfits, revolvers aimed at me. Damien steps forward.

"Give me the Ether device," he commands.

The Rebels react immediately, fear spreading through the crowd as they realize I was telling the truth. The Others are real.

Damien keeps moving toward us. We all begin to step back.

"Ava!" I shout, trying to pull the Ether device from my purse. "Ava, now!"

We keep backing away as Damien and Wendell close in.

Then, in a blur, Ava appears. She leaps onto Damien and strikes him hard in the brachial plexus at the side of his neck. He jerks in pain. Before he can recover, she launches herself at Wendell and hits him the same way. He stumbles, and Ava karate-chops his hand. The revolver slips from his grasp and falls to the ground.

Without hesitation, Ava jumps down and kicks the gun away.

The crowd erupts in cheers.

A gunshot rings out nearby, and a bullet strikes the ground right next to Ava. I know she's in danger as I see Ollie already aiming his revolver at Damien. Damien stares back, trying to predict Ollie's next move. Ollie steps forward, but when Damien tries to do the same, he suddenly stumbles—his boot laces have been tied together. Ava must have done it. Damien trips, and his revolver clatters to the ground. It doesn't fire.

Ollie rushes over and grabs the gun while Damien lies helpless on the ground. I pull out the Ether device and check the coordinates. They're right —this one will take us home. I activate it. The device begins to pulse, and the portal opens with that same stale, strong-smelling air flooding the area.

Ollie and Raquel hold on to me while I carry the picnic basket with Octavius tucked inside my purse. Ava clings to Raquel's back, holding on tightly. I see June running toward us, trying to reach us before we go.

Then, in an instant, I find myself on the floor of my bedroom. We've made it back. Everyone is there—except June.

This time, Ollie and Raquel don't rush to get up. I stay still for a moment too, realizing we left our luggage behind with the Rebels.

"No, we didn't," Ollie says as he stands up. "It's right here." He points to the luggage underneath him. "That's going to leave a mark."

I laugh softly in relief. For now, I don't think the Others know exactly where we are. I could have gone to the orphanage, which might confuse them.

"That's a good point," Ollie says. "But it won't hold them off for long."

He's right. I'm debating whether we should stay here for the night and go looking for Louis in the morning.

"Damien might have had enough for one day anyway," Raquel says, trying to reassure us.

I recall June mentioning the Others in something she said earlier. I turn to Raquel.

"How would she even know about them?"

"Vicki told me a few things," Raquel replies. "She overheard Ms. Collins and Matilda talking and shared it with me. I passed a little of it on to June. Not much. I doubt she believed it anyway."

I nod but keep my thoughts to myself. I'm not sure June was the best person to share that secret with, especially since she's refused to help restore the time continuum. Still, maybe it's harmless. Most people have to see Damien for themselves before they believe any of it. Then again, the more this information spreads, the more tangled and unstable the time continuum becomes.

I go to the refrigerator to see what food is available. Everything has expired.

"I'm not leaving you two alone," I say, glancing at Ollie and Raquel. "Just in case something happens and we get split up."

Even if I gave Ollie an Ether device, keeping one for myself would mean we'd be separated if anything went wrong.

Now that I think about it, we only know one of the coordinates on the second Ether device—the field near the Rebels' settlement.

"Where do the other coordinates even go?" I mutter to myself. "We'll have to figure that out soon."

I decide to order pizza and chicken wings. Oscar deserves a treat, even though I still have a few cans of cat food left for him. We're only staying here for one night at most, so there's no need to go to the grocery store.

A while later, the doorbell rings. I answer it, pay for the food, and bring it to the table. Ollie and Raquel both stare at the boxes like they've seen a magic trick.

"You ordered food... to the house?" Raquel asks.

"Yep. It's called delivery."

They both try pizza for the first time.

"This is incredible," Ollie says with his mouth half full. "What do you call this again?"

"Pizza," I laugh. "And this is Coke," I add, handing them each a cold can.

They take cautious sips and immediately react to the fizz.

"It burns," Raquel says, wincing.

"That's the carbonation. Hang on—I've got lemonade." I go to the fridge, find the lemon concentrate, and make a pitcher of lemonade.

After dinner, we settle into the living room for Bible study, then spend some time praying together. When we finish, I look at Raquel.

"If you want, you can sleep in my room tonight. I have an inflatable guest bed I can use, and you can have the actual bed. That way, Ollie can take the living room."

"Thank you," Raquel says. "That sounds perfect."

I gather the blankets and pillows for Ollie's makeshift bed on the couch.

"Goodnight," I say as I hand him the last pillow.

"Goodnight," he replies, settling in.

I'm also glad Octavius and Ava can finally recharge. I glance over and see them both resting peacefully in their little beds. Ava wears a pink-striped nightcap and lies beneath a soft pink quilt. Her bed frame is cherry wood, and it suits her perfectly.

I make my bed, turn to Raquel, and say, "Goodnight."

"Goodnight," she whispers back.

I lie down, exhausted from the day, and begin to drift off. My thoughts return to June and Vicki. I hope they're alright. I hope this all ends soon.

CHAPTER 12

J wake up to Oscar meowing for his breakfast. I get up and see Raquel is already awake, so I get dressed and head to the kitchen to feed him. After checking on Ava and Octavius, I take them off the charging pad. I'm glad Octavius is fully charged now. I don't expect to be home again for a while.

I put the charging pads away while Ava and Octavius run around the bedroom. Then I go to look for Raquel and Ollie. I notice the front door is slightly open. When I step outside to check, I see them both standing on the balcony, quietly staring out at the city, lost in thought.

I decide to leave them be and glance down at my window boxes. The flowers could use watering. As I tend to them, I start thinking about breakfast. Maybe we could go to a café instead of ordering takeout again. I'm also unsure whether I should return to the museum or visit Louis's house and try to talk to him. I feel indecisive.

"What do you two feel like doing today?" I ask.

Raquel immediately twirls on the glass walkway and shouts, "I want to go to a café!"

I smile. She enjoys being here.

I head back inside to check the house and make sure everything is still in order after being gone. Then I grab our luggage in case we decide to leave today. But as I look around, I realize I'm getting tired and could use a few days of rest now that I'm home. I decide to leave the luggage behind—we can always come back for it if needed.

I also decided to leave Oscar, Octavius, and Ava at home. It might be a little risky, but I don't think the Others will return right away.

I change into my own clothes and pack the dress away in the luggage. Ollie changes, too. As I head to the door, I catch Raquel eyeing my outfit, clearly wanting to wear something like it. I ignore it for now. First, we'll eat. Then we'll talk to Louis.

Whether that conversation leads anywhere, I don't know. But at least it will help us figure out our next step. And maybe, just maybe, we'll get a little rest.

There's a café not far from the house, located in the promenade and tucked beside a cascading waterfall. It's the perfect spot to take Raquel and Ollie. As we make our way there, Raquel looks around curiously, taking in the city sights. When we arrive and she sees the name of the café, she points to the sign.

"Cascade Café," she reads aloud. "That's a very intriguing name."

We sit down at a small table near the window, and a waitress brings us menus. I watch as they study the pages, clearly puzzled. They aren't familiar with most of the items, but they try to find something that looks recognizable.

"What do you two usually like for breakfast?" I ask.

Ollie looks up. "I like meat and a biscuit."

Raquel smiles. "Oatmeal or fruit, if I can get it."

I nod. "Alright. Ollie, try the scrambled eggs with bacon and biscuits with gravy. Raquel, you'll like the fruit bowl and oatmeal. I'll get the strawberry pancakes and some unsweetened iced tea."

The waitress takes our order, and the food arrives shortly after. Everyone enjoys their breakfast. Once we're done, we walk through the city for a bit, window-shopping and taking in the sights.

Eventually, I decide we should make our way to the museum to look for Louis. But I don't want to disrupt Ollie and Raquel's exploring. I figure I'll guide them there without making it obvious, especially since I'm not in a rush to speak with Louis. He might not even have anything to say.

As we stroll along, I suggest, "Why don't we take the metro trams? It'll get us closer to the promenade museums."

Raquel eyes the tram station with curiosity. "Your trains look so much more efficient. But I don't see any steam. Where's it coming from?"

"It's not steam," I explain. "These trams run on magnetic energy. Magnets push against each other with a repulsive force, which moves the tram forward. It's a clean and renewable energy source."

She listens, nodding slowly, though she doesn't look overly impressed. I remind myself that in 1880, concepts like renewable energy weren't part of daily conversation.

We arrive at the museum tram stop, and I say, "Let's head in and look around."

They agree, and we step off the tram. Ollie has been quiet all morning. I'm not sure if he's taking it all in—seeing Sanctuary—or if something's bothering him.

As we walk through the museum doors, a strange feeling washes over me. It's odd being back after so long. I'm not even sure if I still have a job here. For all I know, Ms. Collins may have terminated me for not showing up. Then again, I do have a lot of personal research hours on file. I have no idea what Ms. Collins has told anyone about our disappearance.

I motion for them to follow me as we pass by the main entrance.

"Come on, let's head to my lab."

As we approach the security checkpoint, I reach into my bag and realize something important.

"I forgot my badge," I say, mostly to myself. "Great."

It hits me that forgetting my badge completely defeats the purpose of coming here—to get access to the museum and hopefully find Louis.

We take the elevator, which Ollie and Raquel watch with fascination as it begins to move.

"This is... unusual," Raquel murmurs, glancing at the glowing buttons and smooth ride.

"It's just an elevator," I say, smiling. "It takes us to different floors without stairs."

We reach our floor, and I lead them down the hallway, stopping at the third door on the right—Louis's office. I knock, and to my surprise, he's there, working at his desk. He looks up, startled.

"Oh," he says. "I didn't expect to see you. How's everything going?"

I hesitate. Before I can respond, he keeps talking.

"Ms. Collins told us you went to Arizona, to that Wondering Prospectors mine project. Historical excavation, right? Something about finding evidence tied to the treasure legend. She said you might be helping verify whether it actually existed."

I nod slowly as he talks, pretending to follow along.

"Right," I say. "Actually, I was wondering—do you still have the coordinates for the mine site?"

He stops and gives me a confused look.

"You were on the project," he says. "Shouldn't you already have that? Especially the datum point and GPS location?"

"I need to double-check what the museum has on record," I reply, trying to sound confident. "Just to verify a few things."

He sighs and looks annoyed, but eventually walks over to his filing cabinet. After rummaging through a few folders, he pulls one out and jots down the coordinates on a slip of paper. He hands it to me with an expression that says he doesn't quite trust what I'm up to.

"Thanks," I say, turning toward the door.

As I open it, he follows me out and stops abruptly when he sees Ollie standing there. He does a quick double-take, then steps back.

"Is Ms. Collins adding a living history exhibit to go along with the Arizona mine project?" he asks.

Ollie glances down at his clothes, his expression falling just slightly. He looks both surprised and a little self-conscious. I hadn't thought it would be an issue, assuming people would just assume it was a costume for some theater piece or museum event.

Louis opens the door a little wider to let us pass. That's when he sees Raquel standing just behind Ollie. She's wearing a prairie dress, her hair pinned neatly in a bun. Louis freezes, clearly caught off guard.

"And who is...?" he starts, eyes locked on Raquel. "When exactly is this exhibit supposed to start?"

Raquel, unaware of his stare, leans slightly to peek into Louis's office, her curiosity getting the better of her. Louis watches her, looking more tongue-tied by the second.

Louis offers us coffee and pastries if we'd like to stay and discuss the upcoming event at the museum. Raquel agrees, and I suspect it's partly so she can look around the office more. Louis says he just made a fresh pot of coffee, and he pulls a bottle of creamer from a mini refrigerator behind his desk. There's a small drink station set up with cups and sugar packets.

I've never stayed this long in his office before, and he's never offered me coffee. As he begins talking about how his great-great-great-great-grandfather was a journalist in Arizona before moving to Illinois, something catches my eye. On the left side of his desk, inside a small glass case, I see a little ceramic brown rearing horse—the same one Vicki gave to Philip.

The realization hits me, and suddenly, I feel sad. I want to leave.

Louis continues chatting with Raquel and quickly gathers that she's staying with me for a little while. I wish he didn't know that. She's asking a lot of personal questions, and I worry she might slip up and reveal something that gives away that she's from the past.

After a while, I interrupt and excuse us.

"We need to get going," I say. "We've got to get ready to leave for Arizona soon. Thank you for the hospitality."

Louis nods and asks, "When will you be back?"

"If all goes well," I tell him, "I'll be back at work soon. My guest will be returning to Arizona."

I glance over and see Ollie's face. He looks surprised, even hurt, by what I've just said.

I open the door, and Raquel, unaware of Louis's interest in her, walks out cheerfully. Ollie follows, clearly grumpy. I walk with them down the hall.

"Are you really planning to separate our lives once we stop the Others?" Ollie asks quietly.

I look at him. "I hope not."

He looks down, then turns his gaze away from me. I can see how upset he is at the thought of losing me. No one has ever been that upset about the possibility of my absence before.

Just before the elevator opens, Louis's office door swings open. He steps out and calls down the hall.

"If you like history, there's going to be a hot air balloon event tomorrow! Right in the field outside Sanctuary's entrance. Starts at eleven!"

I look at Ollie and Raquel. They both nod in agreement.

Louis beams. "It'll be a picnic day. Hot air balloon rides and all."

I thank Louis for the invitation just as the elevator opens. Raquel seems excited about the event tomorrow. As I glance at her, I catch Ollie looking at me. Lately, he's been making more eye contact. I notice my palms are a little sweaty, and there's a flutter in my stomach.

We step into the elevator and exit the museum. I'll admit, I'm relieved to still have a job. Everyone seems to think I'm working on a special project for the town. But why would Ms. Collins say that? Why not just terminate me? It almost feels like a setup—or maybe she didn't expect me to return at all. With her version of events, my disappearance wouldn't raise any red flags with the authorities.

I'm starting to see this situation more clearly. The Others appear to be convinced that they can eliminate me, retrieve the Ether devices, and execute their plan for domination. I don't believe Ms. Collins expected me to come back, let alone discover what she's been saying. She may have thought I'd remain in 1880, conveniently out of the way while everything played out.

I feel a heaviness settle over me as we walk home. Through it all, I know God has helped us, keeping us safe, guiding us with clarity. I trust that His will is to restore what's been broken. I believe He'll see us through this.

Raquel and Ollie spend the rest of the day wandering the city and taking in the sights. It really is a beautiful place. But somehow, it doesn't feel the same anymore. It's home, but not home. There's a growing sense of disconnection inside me when it comes to Sanctuary.

After walking most of the day, I decide we should eat out at an all-you-can-eat buffet. This way, Ollie and Raquel can choose whatever they'd like— something familiar or something new. I sit quietly at the table while they explore the buffet, watching them pick out their plates.

My life has revolved around work for so long. It's been ages since I've gone out like this with friends.

Once we return home, we have our Bible study and spend time in prayer. Afterward, I fix tea and relax in the living room. Oscar crawls into my lap, demanding attention, while Ollie and Raquel discover the TV.

Raquel picks up the remote and starts flipping through channels. She keeps changing them nonstop for the rest of the evening, completely fascinated.

I begin to feel sleepy and eventually fall asleep on the couch while watching TV with Ollie and Raquel.

In my dream, I realize I'm lucid. I know I'm dreaming. I find myself walking through an opulent mansion, taking in the lavishly decorated rooms and the spectacular architecture. It feels like I've been wandering for hours.

After a while, I want to leave, but I can't find an exit. I start running through the halls, searching for any outside door. There's nothing. I begin to grow anxious, so I start examining the mansion more carefully, hoping to find clues about who lives here, or maybe discover a secret passage that might lead me out.

At first, the portraits on the walls show beautiful people smiling back at me. But as I move deeper into the house, the images fade. Eventually, the faces are replaced by dark shadows. No eyes, no features, just empty black silhouettes where people once were.

I come to a room with an open window. Long, white sheer curtains float with the wind blowing in from the night air. There's the faint scent of roses. I move closer, thinking I might be able to climb out the window if I'm on the ground floor.

As I approach, I notice a figure behind the curtain. It's waiting there, hidden in plain sight, hoping I won't notice. Against the night sky, it blends in almost perfectly—but I see it. Its long arms, sharp fingers, and pointed nails give it away.

I sense something evil in it.

I turn and run, racing through the mansion. I hear it chasing me, its steps are quick and closing in. My heart pounds. Just before it catches me, I jolt awake.

Ollie looks over and asks, "Are you okay?"

Raquel adds, "You nodded off for a minute."

"It felt so real," I say. "Like I was gone for hours."

It was disturbing—too vivid, too long. I quietly excuse myself and go to bed.

Before I sleep, I pray. I ask God to watch over my body and spirit, to protect me from anything the Others might try while I'm asleep, whether physical or spiritual, like what I saw in the dream.

Oscar hops onto the bed and curls up beside me as I slowly drift off again.

The next morning, Raquel is already up and excited for the picnic. She accidentally wakes me as she gets ready.

"I'm sorry," she says, bright-eyed. "I just can't wait. Can I wear one of your outfits today? I want to fit in a little better."

"Of course," I reply with a yawn.

I help Raquel pick out a long shirt, almost like a tunic, and pair it with a gold belt and cream leggings. I fold her clothes and place them into the luggage. This time, I have a strong feeling we should take our things with us. I bring the picnic basket—not for lunch, but so Oscar can come along. I also carry my purse, with Octavius and Ava tucked safely inside.

I dress in a similar outfit to Raquel's and pack my clothes into the luggage, too. As we're getting ready to leave, Ollie looks at me.

"You look beautiful today," he says with a soft, fake smile.

I notice it immediately. There's something in his tone. I start to get the impression that he thinks I want to return to my old life—that I see all of this as temporary. That's when everything is over; we'll go back to living separate lives. As we leave the house, I find myself thinking more about him, wondering how I really feel, and if I could imagine my life without him now.

I guide us to the tram station. We board and wait quietly as the tram carries us toward our stop. When we arrive, we walk toward the elevators that lead down to the ground level outside the city, similar to our experience during the tour of the ruins.

Before we get on the elevator, Raquel rushes over to the balcony and peers down. She lets out an excited scream.

"I can see them! The tops of the balloons! There are eight of them, all different colors!"

I join her and look down. She's right: the vibrant shapes float gently above the ground. Around us, more people are gathering, many with picnic baskets and multicolored blankets, ready to spend the day enjoying the hot air balloon event.

Raquel glances at the basket and asks, "But what about lunch? Oscar's in the basket."

"There'll be food stands down there," I explain. "Carnival-style food and drinks. We can pick whatever we want once we get there."

The elevator ride feels long, or maybe it's just that I'm genuinely excited. I can't remember the last time I looked forward to an event like this.

As the elevator doors open, I step out and take in the spectacular view. A sea of colorful picnic blankets spreads across the grassy field. Beyond that, the hot air balloons rise in a dazzling wall of color. The scene is lively and chaotic, filled with people walking between rows of booths where street vendors sell food and souvenirs.

I spot Louis waiting for us near the elevators. He walks over with a big smile, though his attention is mainly on Raquel.

"Glad you made it," he says. "It's already a great turnout."

We walked around for a while, stopping at booths to look over the different offerings. After browsing, Louis finds a spot and sets down his picnic blanket. But instead of settling in, he turns to us with a grin.

"Actually," he says, "how about a ride in one of the balloons? My treat. I can get tickets for everyone."

Raquel lights up. She jumps up and down, clapping her hands.

"Yes! Yes! I've always wanted to ride in one of those!"

I glance at Ollie, unsure.

"It's up to you," he says quietly. "If you want to go."

I hesitate. Something about it doesn't sit right with me, but I don't want to split up, and Raquel's joy is infectious. I nod.

"Okay. Let's go."

Still, I can't shake the feeling that this is going to be a wild ride.

CHAPTER 13

*L*ouis leaves to buy the tickets, and Ollie and I stand there for a moment, quietly looking at each other. Raquel, still unaware of Louis's interest in her, is excited and bubbling with energy over the balloon ride.

The scent of fresh pretzels and ice cream drifts through the air, making me realize I'm getting hungry. I decide I'll get something to eat once Louis returns.

"Do you two want anything before we go up?" I ask.

"Ice cream!" Raquel exclaims immediately.

"Same," Ollie says, scanning the area.

They both start searching for a good stand. The variety of flavors overwhelms them—they've never seen so many choices before, especially coming from 1880.

"There's a flavor board on that stand," I point out. "You two go ahead and look. I'll wait here for Louis."

It takes a while, but I know the crowd is thick and Louis is probably hurrying back. Or maybe he just wants an excuse to be near Raquel again. Either way, the extra time gives them a chance to explore the ice cream options without pressure.

As I glance at the flavor list myself, I hear footsteps. Louis is skipping back toward us, holding the tickets in one hand.

"Got them!" he says, beaming.

We walk together to the ice cream stand. I start to pull out my wallet, but Louis quickly steps in front of me and pays for everyone.

"Thank you," Raquel says sweetly.

Louis grins and nods. "Of course."

He walks ahead with Raquel, chatting with her about the ice cream flavors and the booths they've passed. Ollie stays beside me, quiet but present. He ordered two scoops of mint chocolate chip, while I stuck with plain chocolate.

As we walk, I glance sideways and notice the symmetry—Louis next to Raquel, Ollie next to me.

After a while, Louis checks the time. "We've got fifteen minutes to get to the balloons," he says.

"I hope we get the blue one," I tell Ollie. "Blue's my favorite color."

He smiles. "Mine's green. Same color as your eyes. So that works out."

I turn and look at him, grinning as he finishes off his cone.

Up ahead, we see the entrance to the balloon area, marked off by a fence. Behind it, several hot air balloons are lined up and ready. Louis walks up and presents the tickets to the attendant.

Raquel sees a bright yellow balloon and runs toward it with pure joy. I feel a flicker of disappointment—it's not the blue one—but I keep it to myself. She's happy, and I've never seen her light up quite like this.

Raquel runs inside the open door of the wicker basket, and we follow close behind. An attendant approaches and explains the procedures.

"This hot air balloon is fully computer-operated," he says. "We're just going up for a short ride around the dome city and then coming right back down. No need to worry."

We begin our ascent, the burner quietly activating under computer control. Though we haven't risen very high yet, it already feels like we're floating far above the ground. I look over the edge of the basket as we rise, weightless and gliding effortlessly around the dome. Through the glass, I can see faint waterfalls cascading down inside, catching glimmers of light.

I glance over at Ollie. He's smiling, holding the back right rope, clearly enjoying the view. But then his smile fades, and he looks away from the basket, his expression tense. I follow his gaze and notice a shadow slowly creeping over him.

Another hot air balloon is heading toward us.

At first, I assume it's just a technical glitch. Maybe the other balloon has temporarily lost control of its computerized navigation. But it keeps coming closer. I check to make sure the picnic basket with Oscar is secure and give my purse a shake to alert Octavius and Ava.

Then I hear it—a familiar, unsettling laugh. It's wild, manic. I know that voice. The balloon continues closing in, and through its bright blue fabric, I start to realize who's inside.

Louis speaks up.

"Is that balloon going to hit us?"

We're nearly all the way around the dome now. Landing should be happening any minute. I start to relax, hoping this will be over soon. I see a similar look of relief on Ollie's face—until the laugh rings out again, louder, sharper.

I whip my head around.

"Matilda," I say under my breath.

The computerized navigation alarm suddenly blares. We all look up just as the control device begins to melt. Hot plastic and broken components start to drip down onto the basket. I duck, pulling Raquel close. The laughter continues, louder now, and I catch sight of Matilda in her own basket, aiming her balloon directly at ours. She must have used a heat ray to sabotage our system.

Without hesitation, Ollie leaps to the burner and grabs the manual controls. He increases the flame, sending more hot air into the balloon. We begin to rise faster, pulling away from Matilda's path.

I stare at him, surprised.

"I didn't know you could fly one of these."

"I picked it up a while ago," Ollie says, focused. "When it's safe, I'll bring us back down at the event grounds."

I nod, gripping the edge of the basket as we ascend quickly, praying we stay out of her reach.

The laughter returns—faint but still unmistakable. We glance back and see Matilda gaining altitude and speed, closing in on us again. Suddenly, our basket jerks and dips slightly.

I grab the rope next to me. "What was that?"

I turn around and spot a grappling hook lodged into the side of our basket. Matilda has thrown it and is now reeling us in. She's getting closer by the second.

"Why is she doing this?" I mutter. "If we crash, she goes down too."

Before I can say more, Ava runs out onto the rope linking our basket to Matilda's. I shout after her.

"Ava, get back here!"

Octavius follows her out.

Matilda's laugh echoes across the sky as Ava walks the rope like it's a tightrope, balancing with care. But she's not stable. She could fall through at any moment.

Matilda gives the rope a sharp shake. Ava and Octavius nearly fall. I scream.

"Come back! Please, get back now!"

The wind begins to blow harder, adding to the instability. The rope shakes naturally now, making their balance even more precarious.

Ava and Octavius start scooting along the rope, gripping it with both hands. Matilda shakes it again—this time harder. The rope turns into a rolling wave beneath them.

Raquel screams, and I try to think. "There's got to be something we can do."

Ava and Octavius try to turn around, heading back toward us. Matilda lets out a disappointed growl and gives the rope one final, violent shake. Wave after wave rolls toward them as they brace, trying to hold on.

"I can't do anything yet," Ollie says, tense. "We have to wait until they're back in the basket. Then we can cut the rope."

Ava and Octavius get closer, inch by inch.

Suddenly, Matilda drops the end of the rope.

"No!" I cry out.

Ava and Octavius plummet as the rope sways and whips back and forth through the wind.

Without thinking, I lunge forward and grab the rope, pulling hard.

"Hold on!" I yell.

Ollie rushes over and grabs the rope with me. Just then, the grappling hook starts to shake—Matilda is trying to pull it out before we can get Ava and Octavius back into the basket.

Ava shouts up to us, "I have an idea!"

"Whatever it is, it's too risky!" I yell back.

Matilda is pulling her balloon closer as all of this is happening. Without warning, the rope swings toward her, with Ava and Octavius still clinging to it, now swinging toward her basket. They make it just as Matilda gets close and steps into her basket.

Ava distracts her while Octavius grabs the heat ray device and fires it at one of the ropes holding Matilda's hot air balloon. It snaps, and Matilda screams as her basket lurches downward, losing stability. Octavius fires again, hitting the catty-corner rope on the opposite side. The balloon sinks further, rocking violently in the wind.

Matilda screams and rushes toward the burner, trying to land the balloon. Meanwhile, Ava and Octavius leap from her basket, grabbing onto the rope as it swings back through the air. They scream as they sway in the wind.

I go back to pulling them up into our basket. My arms are shaking, and my heart pounds, but we finally get them back in. I sit down, breathless, trying to calm myself. No one says anything at first. We all peer over the edge to see where we are.

I glance back and spot Matilda's balloon continuing to descend.

Then suddenly, our own balloon starts to shake. A familiar, stale smell fills the air.

"She's trying to activate a portal over us," I say.

Everyone looks worried. "We need to land," I suggest.

Ollie nods and begins the descent. The balloon gradually lowers, and we start drifting away from Matilda. I feel some relief as the distance between us grows.

"She's still near us," I tell the group. "We need to think of a plan soon. We don't know what else she might try."

It takes a while, but we finally reach the ground. I see that Matilda has landed to the east.

As we begin discussing what to do next, I turn to Octavius. "What direction are we from Sanctuary?"

"We're northwest of it," he says.

"Good," I reply. "It shouldn't be hard to fly back in the hot air balloon. We need to figure out how to stop Matilda from following us."

I can see Ava deep in thought, clearly trying to figure out how to stop Matilda. I glance toward Matilda's hot air balloon—and it's gone.

"How could it be gone so fast?" I mutter.

"Do any of you see her balloon?" I ask aloud.

Everyone looks around, but no one sees it.

"Wait," I say, narrowing my eyes. "We're not looking high enough."

We all look up. Sure enough, Matilda's balloon is now far above us, high in the sky.

Suddenly, our basket begins to tremble. That stale air smell fills the space around us.

"She activated a portal!" I scream. "It's right over us!"

The basket trembles harder, and then—without warning—it shoots upward into the sky. It feels like we're moving at the speed of light.

The next thing I know, the balloon is falling. The basket shakes wildly in the wind. Ollie scrambles toward the burner, trying to stabilize us. After about a minute, we regain control, though the balloon continues to sway.

We float in silence for a moment.

"Where are we now?" I ask. "What coordinates did she use?"

"Did she send us back to 1880, or somewhere else entirely?" Raquel adds, her voice shaky.

The hot air balloon drifts quietly now, a light breeze brushing past us. No one speaks. Ava and Octavius sit on the edge of the basket, gazing out at the open land below.

"For now, let's just keep going as far as we can toward California," I say. "We'll go until the fuel runs out."

"It won't be long," Ollie says. "We'll need another plan soon."

I scan the land below. "Let's keep an eye out for train tracks. Maybe we can catch a train somewhere. We don't have horses or any other transportation."

For a while, we fly in silence. But I notice the balloon is starting to sink slowly. The sky begins to dim. I hope we find a place to land before dark. My stomach growls.

I say a silent prayer. God, please help us find shelter. We need somewhere safe for the night.

Below us, the landscape stretches out with nothing in sight—just desert. But we keep flying, gradually losing more altitude.

Then, something catches my eye.

"Train tracks," I say, pointing. "Straight ahead."

As we adjust course and begin to follow the tracks, I smile. "Thank you, God," I whisper to myself.

We're barely staying in the air now. The balloon drifts just above the tracks. Far in the distance, I spot a train moving steadily across the landscape.

And then I hear something. A faint singing—soft, male, and distant. I can't tell if it's real or my imagination.

Suddenly, the balloon crashes to the ground next to the tracks. The basket jolts violently, and just beneath us, we all hear a scream.

The hot air balloon is on the ground now. We step out of the basket and begin to survey the crash landing. A smoky smell rises from beneath us, and we realize we've landed right on top of a campfire.

I frown. "Why would there even be a campfire out here? It's broad daylight—and in Arizona."

From just in front of the basket, a man steps forward. His clothes are patched and worn, and he has a tired but friendly smile.

"I'm Anslow," he says. "Didn't expect visitors today."

He seems eager to stay close and offers us some baked beans from a small cooking pot beside a handkerchief tied to a stick—his only belongings.

"Thanks," I say, "but we're good for now."

We're too focused on what's ahead. The hot air balloon has collapsed onto the train tracks, and in the distance, we can hear a train approaching. Anslow glances toward it, then turns back to us.

"So, where are you folks from?"

That gives me an idea. Instead of answering directly, I decide to ask where we are.

"We're thirty miles from hell," he says, laughing. "Just kidding. It's Arizona in 1880. Feels like hell in this heat, though."

Louis lets out a fake laugh and glances at Raquel, clearly hoping for a reaction from her.

At least we know we're in Arizona and still in the 1880s. I'm surprised Matilda didn't send us somewhere worse. Maybe she has a reason for choosing these coordinates. We'll find out soon enough.

As the train gets closer, it begins to brake. The sound is loud and shrill, metal grinding against metal. The conductor and a few other men step off the train and approach us.

"What happened here?" one of them asks.

Ollie, Louis, and a few of the men begin clearing the hot air balloon from the tracks. Louis flexes as he lifts one end of the basket.

"I can clear ten of these off the tracks by myself," he says, throwing a look at Raquel.

Once the tracks are clear, the conductor turns to us.

"Where were you trying to go?"

"California," Ollie says.

"You're headed in the wrong direction," the conductor replies. "But we can give you a ride for about an hour. We'll stop in Red Rock. It's a decent-sized town with hotels, restaurants, and a train station. You should be able to find your way from there."

As we gather our things, Anslow begins following us toward the train. Louis notices and leans in quietly.

"Is this guy coming with us?" he whispers.

I glance at Anslow, carrying his handkerchief-and-stick bag, trying not to look like he's following us at all.

"Yes," I whisper back. "He's stranded out here and doesn't want to admit it."

Louis nods. We'll figure it out when we get to Red Rock. For now, at least Anslow is out of the desert.

We choose an empty train car and settle in. I sit with Ollie along the east wall. Raquel takes a seat against the north side, with Louis following and sitting nearby. Anslow finds a spot on the south wall, already deep into conversation.

"I was working a ranch out west," he begins, his voice full of life. "Held that job for a good stretch, but the owners sold it. Ever since, I've been drifting, hoping to land another ranch job."

He adjusts his seat and continues, "Figured I could cross the desert at night, find shelter during the day, sleep when the sun's high. Thought I could manage it. Turns out, I was wrong."

He chuckles softly, shaking his head.

"I was in the middle of praying when you all came crashing down from the sky. Right on top of my fire. Now if that's not an answer to prayer, I don't know what is."

Louis raises an eyebrow but doesn't say anything. Even he can't argue with that kind of timing.

Anslow leans back and stretches his arms.

"First thing I'm doing in Red Rock is drinking the tallest glass of water I can find. Maybe two."

I glance down at his boots. They're worn through and look uncomfortable at best. Still, he seems unfazed, cheerful even.

"God's good," he says with a nod. "Always comes through in the end."

He grins at us. "If I had a guitar, I'd be strumming it right now. Singing till the sun goes down."

Louis sighs and closes his eyes, clearly done with the conversation.

Then I hear something. A soft thump from the train car behind us. I freeze for a second and glance at Ollie, motioning with my eyes.

He looks at me, then toward the back of the car.

"You hear that too?" he asks quietly.

I nod. "Yeah. We might not be alone."

Ollie shifts his weight and subtly adjusts his position, eyes fixed on the train car door behind us.

Whatever's back there, we're about to find out.

CHAPTER 14

$\mathcal{T}$he train car door is left open by the conductor, giving us a clear view as the train slowly moves along. The desert landscape is beautiful, and Ollie and I sit watching it quietly.

"What are your parents like?" I ask.

Ollie pauses. "My dad's stern and always busy with business. My mom's very independent, likes doing her own thing. They're both pretty hard to get along with. Honestly, they make me want to pull my hair out sometimes."

I wasn't expecting that answer. Ollie is so kind and easy to be around. I guess not everyone turns out like their parents.

Ollie looks at me. "What about your parents?"

"They weren't very affectionate when I was growing up," I say. "They always prioritized their careers. I took a job in another city after school and haven't really thought much about it since. I visit occasionally, and they visit occasionally. I have a brother, but we're not close."

Ollie smiles gently. "I have a brother too. Guess we've got that in common."

I can tell he notices the sadness in my voice. I see a bit of sadness in his eyes as well. The train horn blares, and a cloud of steam passes the open train car door.

From the train car behind us, I begin to hear faint murmuring and a soft banging. Raquel and Louis notice it too. Anslow has his hat pulled low and seems to be napping.

I start to wonder how long we've been traveling and when we'll reach Red Rocks. It feels like at least an hour has passed. The train comes to a sudden halt, and we all glance around.

The conductor walks back toward us.

"There's cattle ahead on the tracks," he says. "It might take a little while to clear them."

He continues past our car, heading to the one behind us to deliver the same update. So there is someone—or several people—back there.

The train remains stopped, and soon I hear footsteps approaching from behind. At first, I assume it's the conductor returning. But as the footsteps draw nearer, I glance up and see two young men peeking into our train car. They wave and greet us with smiles, then quickly strike up small talk with Ollie and Louis.

Anslow wakes from his nap and looks at the two men. His face shows a mix of surprise and anxiety. I could swear he's seen them before, or at least has an idea of what they want.

The men look like they're from a farm, dressed in overalls and straw hats, though they're clean-shaven. Maybe they haven't worked a field in a while. Something about them makes me uneasy.

"Want to play a hand of cards?" one of the men offers.

Louis and Ollie shake their heads.

"We're just passing time," the other man says. "Friendly wager, nothing serious."

Louis responds calmly, "I have no money."

The first man frowns. "No money here?"

Louis repeats, "I have no money here."

They don't seem to understand what he means, but I know he's telling the truth. He has no currency from 1880.

The men exchange a look, slightly annoyed. One of them pulls out a pocket watch.

"Maybe you'd be interested in this," he says, holding it up. There's a subtle, sly grin on his face.

It's obvious they're trying to pull something—rigged card games, stolen goods, maybe both. Their pushiness and fake friendliness give it away.

I start to feel uncomfortable. For a moment, I think maybe I should hand them a little money just to get them to leave. But before I can act, the train lurches and begins to move again—with the men still in our car. I wish the conductor had checked on us before departing, but he probably didn't know they'd moved in while he was clearing the tracks.

I pull my purse close and grip it tightly. The men notice and glance at me, their eyes scanning with interest.

Ollie notices too. He looks down at my purse, then back at the men. He seems to understand I'm protecting the Ether devices, which the men likely think are valuables—cash or jewelry. He shifts slightly, now clearly watching them.

After a tense few moments, the men turn their attention back to Louis and try to strike up a conversation.

Time drags. It feels like another thirty minutes pass as the train glides through the desert. The horn blares again, and clouds of steam rise outside. I can feel the train slowing down. We must be nearing a station. The whistle sounds repeatedly as we roll into the stop, steam clouding the platform and drawing a small crowd of onlookers.

Anslow wakes up just as Louis finishes his conversation with the two men. I feel a wave of relief—we can finally get away from them and find a hotel and a good restaurant. Ollie says he wants to see the train conductor and thank him for the ride and for helping us back in the desert.

I glance at Anslow. He seems nervous, staying close to us. I get the sense he's out of money and scared.

"Would you like to come to dinner with us?" I ask. "It's the least we can do after crashing into your camp."

Anslow smiles. "I'd be delighted."

The two men still hang around at a distance, their eyes lingering on me. They must think I have something incredibly valuable in my purse. And I do. I shudder to think what they would do with an Ether device—if they even figured out how to use it.

Raquel has been quiet for a while. I notice her window shopping as we walk through the town of Red Rock. The main road is wide, with small wooden shops scattered along both sides. There's no covered porch walkway like in Rocky Creek, and the town feels smaller, less prosperous.

We make our way to the only large restaurant and hotel in town. It sits near the center, with the mine off to the left and a small church at the far end of the road.

"Too bad it's Friday and not Sunday," Ollie says as he glances toward the church.

I smile faintly. I had nearly forgotten what day it was. Part of me wishes we were back in Rocky Creek with Vicki, enjoying a quiet day instead of running from the Others and trying to foil their plans. I wonder what will happen to the hot air balloon left behind on the train tracks.

The restaurant has a menu nailed to the front door. As we look it over, I notice the two men again, watching from afar.

"Let's head inside and get a table," I say quietly.

Many restaurants in my time try to imitate rustic charm, but this one is the real thing. The interior is warm and simple, with wooden tables and a faint scent of wood smoke in the air.

The meal is delicious. Most of us order the steak with mashed potatoes —the daily special. We're in no hurry to leave, and we all decide to stay for dessert. The walnut cake is rich and pairs perfectly with hot tea.

After we finish eating, Ollie gets up to ask about rooms for the night. We both agree it's safer to check into the hotel and stay off the streets. Better to rest somewhere secure than risk another encounter with those men.

Ollie has gotten us three rooms. He places two room keys on the table. Louis looks at him and asks, "Where are you sleeping?"

"I'll take the single bedroom," Ollie says. "Raquel and I will share a double, and so will the rest."

Louis glances at Anslow and scowls. "That isn't fair. Just because I don't have any money right now to get my own room, I have to share with a stranger?"

He quickly adds, "Let's do a coin toss. Or better yet—rock, paper, scissors."

Ollie shakes his head. "There are only three rooms left tonight. We were lucky to get them at all."

Louis frowns. "Why is a town in the middle of nowhere all booked up?"

"There are bigwigs from the mine headquarters in town," Ollie says. "I don't know the details, but it has something to do with the mine."

Louis still pushes for the coin toss, but Ollie ignores him and walks away, leaving the two room keys on the table. He heads to the counter to pay for the meal.

Anslow looks relieved. He's grateful just to have a place to stay for the night. I feel a bit sorry for him, but he carries himself with such gratitude and peace, thanking God for everything he has.

Raquel and I head up to our room. The waitress smiles and tells us she'll send up complimentary tea and pastries this evening, if we'd like. Anslow quickly accepts, and Raquel nods as well.

The hotel is surprisingly fancy. The hallway is dressed with a Cadet gray runner, patterned rugs, and beautiful floral wallpaper with gold highlights. The room itself matches the décor downstairs—elegant wallpaper, soft curtains, and a richly colored area rug.

The beds are made with solid gold-colored bedspreads, crisp white sheets, and pillowcases. The room is plain in layout, with just the beds, a stand, and a small dresser, but the details make it feel refined.

Later, the waitress brings up the tea cart. We enjoy the pastries, though I wish I had skipped dessert earlier.

Raquel grins and says, "We only live once. Who knows when we'll get to enjoy pastries like these again?"

There's a knock at the door. It's Louis, coming to chat with Raquel. Anslow follows close behind and begins sharing stories from his days on the ranch.

I suggest a Bible study, and before I know it, Louis is nowhere to be found. Anslow knocks on Ollie's door to invite him. After we pray together, the evening winds down. We're all tired and ready for a good night's sleep.

I wake up to the morning sun streaming through the window. After getting dressed, I head down for breakfast. Since checkout isn't for a while, we leave our things in the rooms. I grab my purse, just in case.

Breakfast is wonderful—pancakes with maple syrup and a pot of hot tea. I savor the calm, though I feel unsure about what comes next. We have no clear plan.

"I think we should meet in one of the rooms," Ollie says. "We're not running from anything for once, so let's focus and make a plan for dealing with the Others."

We all agree. But when we return to our floor, I notice something immediately wrong. The door to our room is ajar. I know I locked it.

I push the door open slightly and peek inside. Two men are inside, ransacking the room, digging through our things—clearly searching for whatever they think is in my purse.

Louis spots me at the doorway and, in the loudest voice possible, says, "Stop creeping around the door!"

He laughs, unaware of the situation. I raise my hand to my mouth, and he stops laughing. He realizes something is wrong.

The men hear Louis and look straight at the door. They see me and immediately move toward it. One of them throws it open, and I stumble back. He lunges for my purse. I kick him in the chin.

Ollie draws his revolver. The two men pull theirs in response.

One of them smirks. "Well, look at that. You're outgunned here, aren't you?"

My purse begins to shake in my arms. I clutch the top tightly, trying to keep Octavius and Ava from bursting out. The shaking grows more violent. The men take notice.

"What's going on in there?" one of them asks.

I say nothing. I can barely hold onto the bag.

Without warning, the purse jerks out of my grip and smacks one of the men in the face. He stumbles back with a shout. The purse strikes him again, harder this time. He screams and aims his revolver at me, stepping forward.

But as he moves, he trips and crashes to the floor. His shoelaces are tied together.

The other man lunges toward me, maybe trying to grab me as a hostage, but Ollie quickly pulls me back and shields me. Suddenly, the man yells, calling out for someone—backup, maybe.

Ollie leans in and whispers, "It's time to go."

I know exactly what he means. I reach into my purse and grab one of the Ether devices.

The man catches sight of it and reaches for it. "So this is what all the fuss is about," he sneers.

I kick him hard in the chin as the rest of us start backing away—everyone except Anslow and Louis. Raquel yells for them to get closer. At that moment, another man steps out of a nearby room, revolver drawn. He must have been hiding there while the others tore through our room.

I press the button on the Ether device. It begins to pulse in my hand. Anslow looks panicked.

"What's happening?" he shouts.

Before I can answer, the familiar stale air hits us, and everything blurs. We slam to the ground. It takes a moment for us to gather ourselves and look around.

The hotel is gone.

I sit up slowly, confused, trying to make sense of where we've landed. Then it hits me—I must have grabbed the Ether device we got from Matilda. The coordinates must have been reversed during the scuffle, and the time input is off. I estimate we've been sent back about twenty-five years.

I glance around again. The town looks familiar, just stripped back—no hotel, no restaurant, fewer buildings.

I think back to Louis's conversation at the museum and realize something: the reversed coordinates from the Rebel settlement might point directly to the mine the Others were interested in. But I didn't expect it to land us in 1855. Could this be when the Others are targeting the mine?

Our luggage, of course, is still sitting in the hotel room in 1880. I consider going back for it, but we don't know how to reset the time on the Ether device.

I feel helpless.

Anslow sees the look on my face and says calmly, "Don't worry. God will provide."

We take a few tentative steps through the town. It's recognizable primarily, but quieter, emptier, rougher. We begin searching for anything useful—a train schedule, a clue, a direction.

Anslow approaches a window displaying a few tattered papers. He reads one and suddenly shouts with excitement.

"There's a job opening nearby," he says. "Helping a prospector."

"Where is it?" I ask.

"Red Mountain," he replies.

Something clicks in my memory—the legend of the wandering prospector's fortune. I'd heard it before—how he lived and worked around Red Mountain and supposedly buried his treasure somewhere in the hills.

I agree with Anslow—we should at least go. The chance that the Others are showing up at the same time as the Wandering Prospector is too much of a coincidence to ignore.

Ollie says, "It's probably a few miles away. If we're taking Anslow there, we should get going so we can be back in Red Rock by noon."

"Why noon?" I ask.

"To investigate the mine," he replies.

Now I understand what he's thinking, and I nod in agreement. "Let's get moving."

Red Mountain rises to the right of town, looming in the distance. Its straight, sheer sides lead up to a jagged, wild summit. It looks dangerous, even deadly. People have lost their lives trying to climb it, chasing the legend of the buried treasure. I stare at the mountain and think you'd have to be crazy to attempt it.

As we walk, we pass several pack mules headed in the same direction. They're not going to the main mine—they're headed toward Red Mountain. That catches my attention. Maybe the Others aren't focused on the known mine. Maybe there's another one in the mountain itself.

We keep walking over the desert ground, patchy with shrubs and dry grass. The morning coolness is quickly giving way to the unforgiving heat. I start to feel it—the boredom of walking, the heavy sun, the dryness.

After a while, I stumble a little, and Ollie looks at me.

"You okay?" he asks. "We've only been walking about fifteen minutes."

Anslow chimes in. "We could try to find a cactus and slice a branch. You can get water out of them."

"There aren't any cactuses out here," Ollie says. "But we're almost there. We can ask for water when we get there."

Eventually, we come to a small wooden structure nestled against the base of the mountain, just off the trail from town. It's hard to tell what it is —maybe a house, maybe an old supply store. It could have been an office for a long-closed mine. Whatever it was, it hasn't been used in a while.

I glance at the faded job posting Anslow found and sigh. "We might be twenty years too late for this job inquiry."

We all stand there for a while, silent, unsure what to do next. Just as we start to turn back toward town, a loud voice calls out from behind.

"Hey! Get off my lawn!"

We spin around to see a man standing not far from us, grinning as he watches our startled reaction.

"Just Arizona humor," he says, clearly amused.

He steps closer. "So, what brings you all out to Red Mountain?"

CHAPTER 15

*A*nslow greets the man and explains that he saw a job advertisement for help around the place. He admits the job description was vague, but mentions he's a professional cattle rancher. The man looks at Anslow, smiles, and says, "I've got a small farm."

Anslow glances around and asks, "Where's the farm located?"

The man replies, "We'll go over the final details later on."

Anslow looks a little disappointed. "When might I hear back about the job?"

"Come back this afternoon for a formal interview," the man says.

Anslow agrees, and we decide to head back to town. I get the feeling this man hasn't had many people ask about the job, but something about this mountain feels off to me.

As we walk, it starts to hit me: the Others might be interested in this mine because the minerals here could be components for Ether devices. That idea gives me a new perspective. Maybe they're planning to produce more of them.

Ollie carries the picnic basket with Oscar in it, helping me out. I glance back and notice the man still watching us from a distance. He seems intuitive, like he can read us and get a feel for who we are. I get the sense he doesn't trust easily and stays cautious.

My curiosity grows. Why were those pack mules headed to Red Mountain? Could there be treasure up there—maybe gold? I also realize we never asked for water while we were there. By the time we get back to town, we're thirsty, so we stop at a small restaurant and each get a big glass of water.

While sitting there, I do a double-take when I see a woman walking past the window. Is that Ms. Collins?

Then, a few minutes later, I catch sight of someone else. It looks like Wendell. I excuse myself from the table.

"I'll be right back," I tell the group as I quietly follow Wendell.

Sure enough, he heads toward the mine. I watch from a distance as he stops and begins talking to Ms. Collins. Both are dressed in clothing that fits in perfectly with 1855. There's a third person there, standing with his back to me. I get a feeling I already know who it is. Then he turns just enough for me to see a patch of gray skin under his wide-rimmed floppy hat.

I know it's Damien.

They're at the mine here in Red Rock. I don't know if Red Mountain is connected to the Others and their plans. I want to get closer and figure out what's going on, but for now, I should head back before the group realizes I've been gone too long—or worse, one of the Others spots me.

My purse starts to shake. I quietly call for Octavius, and he peeks out. He scans the area and says, "I don't like this situation."

"Why not?" I ask.

He frowns. "The mine is officially registered. So how are they getting access to it? Maybe they're pretending to be employees or potential buyers. But where are the actual mine workers? Why are the Others here when no one else seems to be around?"

He's right. Something feels off. We need to get back before we're noticed.

Ava suddenly whispers, "Wait. Don't turn around yet. Keep your head down."

A minute passes, and then Matilda walks right by us. If I'd headed back toward the restaurant just a moment earlier, I would have run right into her. I turn quickly once she's passed. Matilda must be deep in thought—I'm surprised she didn't notice me, especially with my purse in plain sight.

I hurry back to the restaurant and sit down just as everyone else is getting up.

"Where are we going?" I ask.

Ollie shrugs. "We're not sure yet. Maybe we should check out the mine."

I blurt out, "Maybe we should explore more of the town first."

They look at me, a little puzzled, sensing something's off. I know I'm acting strange and stalling, but I can't help it.

Just then, a young woman walks through the center of town wearing pants and traditional cowboy gear, fitted for a woman. Her long black curls bounce with each step, and her light blue eyes stand out even from a distance. Ollie spots her and immediately lowers his head, turning away. He keeps his hat down and sneaks a glance back to make sure she didn't notice him.

I don't know who she is, but Ollie clearly does—and this is twenty-five years before his own time. I start to wonder about his life, who he's known, what he's been through. The woman was striking, almost as beautiful as Raquel.

As the group starts walking toward the mine, I blurt out a question that's been on my mind. "Why didn't the Ether device affect you the same way? Why weren't you pulled back through time like we were?"

I know I'm delaying again, but I need to know.

Anslow glances at me and replies, "I guess I was displeased with where I was anyway."

It makes sense that the group heads toward the mine again. Once we turn the corner past the last building on the right and walk closer, we realize all the Others are gone. I wonder where they went—maybe they're inside the mine now.

There's a business-looking man who steps out of a small building near the entrance. He sees us and calls out, "You folks new to town?"

Anslow replies, "I hope so. I'm hoping to get a job over at Red Mountain."

The man looks intrigued. "Why do you want to work there?"

"It's a good job," Anslow says.

The man studies him for a moment. "What kind of work will you be doing?"

"Mostly helping out," Anslow replies.

The man looks at him, a bit speechless at the vague answer.

I step in and ask, "What are the pack mules at Red Mountain for?"

The man responds, "There's a farm out that way. The mules bring in potatoes and leafy greens. I've even heard rumors of a few date and pecan trees. Maybe even some cotton. No one knows for sure, though. The farm's location is a bit of a secret."

Anslow asks, "Have you ever wondered where it is?"

"There are a lot of secrets Red Mountain keeps to itself," the man says, half smiling.

Then he asks, "So when's your interview?"

"This afternoon," Anslow says. "Not exactly sure what that means, but that's when it is."

The man nods. "Sounds like Benjamin Loughry."

He looks at all of us. "Do you have a place to wait until then?"

Anslow shakes his head. "We don't."

"Well, you're welcome to wait in the mine office lobby," the man offers. "There are some books, and we've got tea and pastries. Or if you'd rather, we can make some lemonade with the few lemons we've got left. My name's Leon."

We all greet him, and he adds, "At least you'll be out of the sun while you wait."

We thank him as he heads off, and we step inside the office. The room is warm and inviting, with a few sofas and a coffee table in the center. Bay windows let in the light, and dusty blue drapes match the sofas nicely. Along the back wall is a snack station of sorts, with a tea cart and a display offering sugar cookies and slices of walnut cake. To the left, there's a door leading to an indoor plumbing restroom.

Everyone goes for the walnut cake and tea. As I enjoy the unexpected treat, I think it's very kind of the man to offer us a place to stay while we wait.

After we eat, everyone drifts toward the bookshelf near the front door. I glance to the left and notice the office, which holds several filing cabinets and two roll-top desks. One is locked shut. The other is open, its surface visible.

As I walk by, something catches my eye—a list of names. I lean in slightly. There it is: Damien and Wendell. My stomach sinks. That can't be a coincidence. Did the man already know who we were? Was this a trap? Or did he really not know and offer us kindness without any hidden motive?

I look over at Ollie, who's been quiet ever since we arrived in Red Rock. He hasn't said much, especially after seeing that woman walk by earlier. I know he recognized her, but I still don't know what their history is.

I take another glance at the open desk, trying not to draw attention. That's when I spot it—a check made out by Damien to someone named Leon. My heart sinks again.

"I hope that's not a payoff to get into the mine," I mutter under my breath.

Ollie doesn't respond. He's reading something, eyes far away like he's somewhere else entirely. I sit back down, sip my tea, and stare out the window. Then I go ahead and take a second slice of walnut cake.

Time passes slowly. It's well past noon when Ollie finally sets his book down.

"We should take a long lunch," he says. "Then head over to see this Benjamin Loughry."

"Sounds good," I reply. "We can get to the restaurant early."

At lunch, I look across the table at him. "I'm glad it's Saturday," I say. "We can go to church tomorrow morning."

I wave the waiter over. "Do you know what time the service starts?"

"Ten o'clock," he says with a polite nod.

I glance at Ollie, and he gives a small smile. I can tell he's glad, too. I think the only one who might not show up is Louis—unless he decides to go just to be with Raquel.

After lunch, we sit under the awning outside. It's cooler here than inside. A warm breeze passes through, and the shade feels good. We rest for a while and ask for a glass of water before we head off toward Red Mountain

After we finish our water, we gather for a group prayer, asking that Anslow get the job—if it's God's will for him to have it. When we stand up, we begin the walk toward Red Mountain. The sun feels hotter than it did earlier, but at least this time we're well-fed for the journey.

We return to the spot where we first saw Benjamin Loughry, but he's not there. I figure his idea of "afternoon" might be different from ours. I walk up to the building and peek through the windows. It looks like an office, an odd structure built right up against the mountain itself.

I knock on the door, but there's no sign of anyone inside. From what I can see through the glass, the place is empty.

Anslow turns to us. "Maybe y'all should go find a room for tonight. I'll stay here and wait."

Louis jumps on the idea. "Sounds good to me. Let him wait while we check in."

I shake my head. "I don't think we should split up. Just this morning, if I had run into Matilda alone, I might've used the Ether device and gotten separated from all of you."

Before the conversation goes any further, the office door creaks open. Mr. Loughry steps outside. I look at him, confused. I'm sure there wasn't anyone inside just a minute ago. I glance at the building again. It's backed right up against the mountain—how did he get in there?

Anslow and Mr. Loughry step aside to talk privately. I watch their exchange. It's hard to read, but I get the sense that it didn't go terribly. At least Anslow gave it a shot

Now we can return to town, get a hotel, and start looking seriously into what's going on with the mines.

Louis suddenly looks off to the east, eyes wide. I follow his gaze and freeze. A giant wall of sand is sweeping toward us.

Ollie points. "It's a haboob!" he shouts.

I don't know exactly what that is, but I can guess—it means we're about to get swallowed by a massive sandstorm.

Benjamin looks over at us, probably trying to decide if there's time to make it back to town. Just then, the young woman from earlier appears. She looks older now and calls out to Ollie.

"Come inside, quick!" she says, already heading toward the office.

We don't hesitate. With the sandstorm racing toward us, we follow her in. She walks straight to a bookcase against the back wall and pushes it aside. Behind it is a hidden passage. She reaches to a shelf on the left side and grabs a modern flashlight, switching it on. Then she tosses another one back to Ollie.

"Take this," she says.

He catches it, and we all begin moving into the narrow, dark cave. Behind us, I hear Benjamin slide the bookcase shut. The passage is long and winding, and the walls feel close, but we keep going, the sound of the storm fading behind us.

We walk for a while until we reach a circular, room-like structure where natural light streams in from a gap high up on the mountainside. It's not the peak, which must be several thousand feet up, but still high enough that the light feels distant. The woman walks up to one section of the cavern wall and begins feeling around. I have no idea what she's looking for—until her hand suddenly goes through the rock. That's when I realize it's not solid. It's a holographic projection, disguising a natural cave entrance hidden behind the illusion of stone.

Just before stepping through, she glances at Ollie and catches him watching me while I watch her. She gives a small nod, then leads the way through the opening. We follow, emerging into what can only be described as a cave house. The room we enter looks like a cozy living room, filled with furniture that looks straight out of the 1920s—an upright piano, armchairs with floral upholstery, and rich wood accents. Natural skylights cut through the stone ceiling, bathing everything in a soft, diffused glow.

I can't help but wonder, what happens when it rains? Just as the thought crosses my mind, the woman answers it, as if reading it from me.

"If it rains, a hologram security feature activates," she says. "It forms a hard surface over the openings to keep out the rain—and things like a haboob."

I glance to the right and see a small modern kitchenette. A dishwasher hums quietly next to a washing machine. No wonder Benjamin didn't want us coming inside. This place practically radiates Ether device energy, and there it is, one sitting prominently on the counter.

The woman turns to us. "My name is Lydia," she says.

Just then, a chubby woman with light brown curly hair and light eyes appears from another room off to the far right. She looks genuinely surprised to see us. Benjamin stands nearby, tall and thin, with dark, straight hair and eyes. I get the sense that the younger woman is their daughter. She's tall and slim, with her mother's curly hair and eyes, but her hair is the same dark shade as Benjamin's.

This isn't just a house; it's a cave mansion. I find myself curious about the rest of it. Are other rooms decorated in different historical periods? The living room feels carefully styled in a Roaring Twenties theme, down to the details. A large floral area rug covers the center of the room, and for a moment, I think of Ollie's rugs—the ones he makes himself. There's one here in the same style, and though it's slightly out of place in the 1920s decor, it's still charming.

And unmistakably, it's Ollie's work. His rugs have found their way here.

I ask Ollie, "Have you ever sold any of your rugs?"

He looks at me and shrugs. "Nope."

Lydia, standing nearby, is discreetly listening. She's always taken an interest in Ollie and me whenever we're together.

Just then, Benjamin looks toward the nearest skylight. "Has the haboob passed yet?" he asks.

The chubby woman, who had surprised us earlier, steps closer and smiles. "We might as well let them stay the night," she says to Benjamin. "They've already seen the secret home. We've got two guest rooms. Dinner will be ready in about three hours."

She turns to us. "I'm Fleur," she says warmly.

Fleur leads us down a long hallway—the same one she'd first emerged from, which I had assumed led to just one more room. At the end are the guest bedrooms. They're much simpler than the main living space, small and neat, each with two narrow beds, a small stand in the center, and an armoire against the back wall.

She glances down at the picnic basket in my hands. "What's in there?"

I open it carefully. "Oscar."

She peers inside and smiles. "Has he eaten recently?"

"I've been giving him scraps from my meals," I say.

Fleur nods and gently takes the basket. "I'll put him in a small room with food and find some sand for a litter box."

"Thank you," I say, genuinely touched by her kindness.

She smiles again. "Do you have any luggage?"

"We got separated from it," I explain.

Fleur waves a hand. "No problem. I'll bring a few dresses and things Lydia hasn't worn in years."

Raquel and I both thank her. I sit on the first bed to rest for a moment, thinking back to what Fleur said about the two guest rooms. One is clearly for Raquel and me. I assume the other is for Louis and Anslow. But then— why wasn't Ollie mentioned as a guest? And why is Lydia so interested in him?

I ponder this quietly while Raquel twirls around the room, admiring everything. "This house is amazing," she says. "And Lydia and Fleur are just the sweetest."

I nod, but my mind is elsewhere.

CHAPTER 16

As time passes, I start to feel a little hungry and find myself thinking about exploring more of the cave. I also begin to wonder where Ollie is. I'll ask him later about checking out the rest of the cave. I know dinner must be close because I can smell steaks and mashed potatoes cooking. The delicious aroma only makes my hunger worse.

Fleur knocks on the open bedroom door and lets us know that supper is ready. Raquel and I head toward the living room, pass through the kitchen, and enter another room located just behind it. The dining room entrance is set into the back wall of the kitchenette. The room is beautiful, with a large black table bordered in colorful tile and matching black chairs. In the center of the table sits a flower arrangement made of plastic white lilies. I've always loved lilies. Sometimes I like them even more than roses, though it's a tough choice.

Raquel and I pick our seats, and a moment later, Ollie arrives and takes the one next to mine. Lydia comes in, and almost instantly, I smell the same floral scent I noticed the first day I met Damien. It's her perfume.

"Whoever is wearing perfume has a charming scent," I say aloud.

Lydia smiles. "Thank you. It's made from Chinese peony. It's a little like rose but sweeter."

Raquel seems to take note of the comment about Lydia's perfume. Fleur gathers everyone and has us take our seats as dinner is served. Anslow places his napkin across his shirt like a bib. Ollie casually mentions, "Church starts at 9:30 tomorrow morning."

I'm glad. I've been looking forward to attending church, and it'll be a unique experience, going back to 1855 in such a setting.

After dinner, I turn to Ollie. "Can we explore the cave a little?"

He nods. "You and Raquel can take a look, but most of it's not much for sightseeing. The house doesn't go far beyond what you've already seen. The rest is just empty cavern space."

Benjamin adds, "Living in a cave is better in Arizona anyway. It stays cool in the summer, and you don't have to deal with the damage from heat and sun like a regular house."

I ask him, "Why do you have the office building?"

He explains, "It came with the property when I bought it from the mine across town. The original plan was for the mine to be here, in Red Mountain. They even named it the Red Mountain Mine. But the mine only had luck at the very front. That's where they found some minerals, but not much else. So they shut it down and relocated the operation."

He pauses, then continues. "Maybe there's more here, but it wasn't worth the cost or risk to keep digging. The outer mountain is dangerous, and the miners have already scoured it. All they really found was a natural spring beneath it."

I ask Benjamin, "Why did you leave the office building standing instead of tearing it down?"

He sighs. "People have been breaking into it since the day we got here. Always snooping around the mountain, spinning stories about us having some kind of hidden fortune."

I look at him, puzzled. "Why would they think that?"

He nods toward the living room. "The only fortune I've got is inside that little treasure chest on the bookcase."

Still confused, I ask, "But where did the idea come from? Why do people think you're sitting on treasure?"

Benjamin explains, "Fleur wrote a series of pioneer cookbooks. They sold well—really well, in general stores all over the country. Around that same time, I was out in California panning for gold. I didn't find much, but while I was gone, Fleur's books were taking off. So when we came back with enough money to start a cattle ranch in her hometown, folks just assumed we'd struck it rich. Add in the fact that we ended up buying Red Mountain, and people filled in the blanks."

I nod slowly. "But the mountain was abandoned, right?"

He chuckles. "Exactly. The property was cheap—just an old mine, left for sale. No one wanted it."

Still, something doesn't add up. "It just seems strange," I say. "Starting a cattle ranch but living far away from it, staying here at Red Mountain where there's... not much."

Benjamin shrugs. "It works for us."

Ollie speaks up. "Why don't we go check out that natural spring under the mountain?"

I perk up. "That sounds great."

He and I stand, and I turn to Raquel. "Wanna come?"

She smiles. "Of course."

Ollie leads us back through the living room and into the circular cave room again. From there, he guides us to a corridor on the far side. He clicks on a flashlight, and we begin to walk. I can tell we're going downhill—the ground is growing damp and a little slick beneath our feet. The walls glisten with moisture, and the air is getting colder the farther we go.

Eventually, the corridor opens into a room where a small pond rests quietly. This is where the spring emerges. Thin beams of natural light filter faintly into the cave through gaps above us. The room is beautiful. The water looks clean and cold, refreshing enough to drink, especially in the Arizona heat.

"Are there more places to explore?" I ask Ollie.

"There are," he says. "But maybe later."

He must see the disappointment in my face, because he pauses. "There's a nice room off this chamber that leads back up toward the house. Want to see it?"

Raquel's eyes brighten. "Yes, let's go!"

Ollie smiles and guides us toward another corridor that branches off from the spring room.

On the way, I swear I hear murmuring up ahead. I glance at Ollie. "Does anyone else have access to the mountain?"

He gives me a curious look. "Why do you ask?"

"Just listen," I say. "It sounds like people are ahead of us down the corridor."

Ollie stops in his tracks and listens. The faint murmuring reaches his ears, too. His posture stiffens.

"Let's take the other way back," he says quietly. "I'm not sure who else is here. The Others may have the cave coordinates, too."

Concern creeps in as we start heading back. The murmuring grows louder and shifts into whispering. The ground is slick with condensation, too slippery to run. I pick up a small rock and toss it toward the sound.

The whispering stops.

They know we're here.

Ollie waves for me to keep moving. I glance back, half-expecting someone to appear from the darkness.

We reach the circular cave room and stop to catch our breath. The silence holds, and for now, it seems we've lost whoever was there. Ollie guides us through the hologram, back into the hidden house. As we walk, I start to wonder how Ollie knows so much about this mountain.

Who is *Ollie, really?*

That evening, we gather for a group Bible study. Afterward, Fleur plays the piano and sings a mix of hymns and old songs. My favorite song she plays is "Come Where My Love Lies Dreaming." My favorite hymn is still "Amazing Grace."

Ollie picks up a guitar that rests beside the piano and begins strumming along with Fleur. I watch him, struck by how content he looks here. I want what he has—a sense of belonging, a family, a place that feels like home.

I glance around the room. Raquel is smiling as she sings. Louis tries out silly voices to make her laugh. I don't know much about Anslow yet, but I can tell he's someone who doesn't have anyone waiting for him either.

The evening drifts by peacefully. Eventually, the music winds down, and we all go to bed.

The next morning, Fleur makes us pancakes with bacon and eggs. As she pours orange juice, she grins.

"I have a special treat for you all," she says. "This juice is fresh from California."

The taste instantly reminds me of the plan Ollie and I once had—to leave for California and stay at his cousin's stump house. But now, I'm beginning to wonder if that plan will ever happen. What does the future hold for Ollie and me?

After breakfast, we get ready for church. We leave the mountain and exit through the office building. In the distance, a few townspeople turn and watch as we emerge. Their expressions carry a mix of curiosity and quiet disapproval. The people of Red Rock seem both intrigued by and resentful of the Loughrys.

The walk back into town is more pleasant with the cooler morning air. I left Oscar, Octavius, and Ava behind at the house. I miss them already and hope to spend more time with them later today or tomorrow.

As we walk through the town, not much seems to have changed. But when we reach the church, I immediately notice a difference. In 1880, the church appeared newly constructed. This older version is stunning in its own way. A white stucco wall surrounds the property, with a wooden gate set into it. Above the gate is a decorative stucco arch, topped with a simple cross. Some areas of the stucco have chipped away, revealing the original brickwork underneath.

The landscape around the church is just as lovely, filled with desert plants—cacti, succulents, and even a few blooming flowers. We walk through the gate and into the courtyard. The chapel itself is made of white stucco with patches of exposed brick. Its front doors are arched and wooden, and like the gate, a small stucco cross rests at the top where a steeple would generally be.

Inside, the church opens into a large, peaceful room. The floor and ceiling are both made of the same white stucco. Two rows of wooden pews run down the center, leading up to a small pulpit close to the front row—no microphones, of course, at this time.

The church is already filling up. A woman near the front waves Fleur over to sit beside her. I follow, unsure of where I should go. Benjamin trails behind Ollie. There's not enough space for all of us, so Raquel, Louis, and Anslow find a pew a few rows back as others continue to fill the room.

The sermon is centered around a verse that immediately holds my attention: Psalm 1:3 — "And he shall be like a tree planted by the rivers of water, that bringeth forth his fruit in his season; his leaf also shall not wither; and whatsoever he doeth shall prosper."

As I listen, I'm reminded of the dream I had—the one where a shallow, peaceful river turned into something dark and dangerous. I remember how a vine pulled me toward deep, murky water, away from the canoe, and into a chaotic, unnatural current.

I BELIEVE that dream was a warning. That vine was Satan, trying to pull me off course—to take away what's been given to me. My salvation.

I begin to realize just how important it is to have a personal relationship with Christ. Being left to navigate the dangerous waters of life alone only leads to destruction. I glance over at Ollie. He looks deep in thought, fully focused on the sermon.

My eyes wander to the right corner of the church, where a large angel statue stands. I stare at it for a while, taking in its presence. Next to it, mounted on the wall, is a wooden cross with a small image of Christ nailed to it. The sight brings back memories of my dream—the one with the shadowy figure chasing me through a mansion.

I think about that dream again, trying to make sense of it. The cave mansion we stayed in only has a small house within it, so it couldn't be the one from the dream. And while I don't remember Satan ever being described as having a mansion in the Bible, I do know he is called the ruler of this world. He uses distraction—fame, money, power, even love and family—to pull people away from God's will.

A heavy feeling starts to settle over me. Was that dream a warning? Is Satan trying to distract me with the desire for a big family, knowing how much I want that?

Sadness creeps in as I wrestle with the thought.

Just then, I hear the pastor quote Psalm 37:4: "Delight thyself also in the Lord: and he shall give thee the desires of thine heart."

The verse settles in my heart like a calm after a storm. I know what I need to do. If I put God first, He will lead the way—and if it's His will for me to have a large family, it will happen in His timing. The sadness begins to lift.

I glance back at Ollie. He's still lost in thought. When he notices me looking at him, he gives a small, forced smile.

After the sermon ends, I take a few moments to look around the church. Fleur and Leon are speaking with friends, and Ollie joins the conversation. Raquel follows along with me while Louis and Anslow get caught up talking with the people they sat beside.

Near the front door, I spot another statue—this one of Christ seated with several children around Him. There's a quiet, gentle beauty to it. I've come to appreciate the presence of statues in a church. There's something comforting about them, something reverent. I find myself wishing modern churches in 2280 still had them.

Ollie joins us, and we step outside to explore the church garden. It's peaceful, with clusters of pink Desert Rose and Adenium Roses, along with vibrant scarlet Hedgehog Cactus blooming brightly under the morning sun. As we walk, I notice a few more statues scattered among the plants.

One in particular catches my attention—an angel with her wings spread wide and a horn in her hand. I walk over for a closer look. Ollie is nearby, still admiring the flowers. When I glance back at the statue, I see something that wasn't there before: a wide-rim floppy hat resting on the angel's head.

My heart skips.

I glance around, suddenly alert. The air carries that unmistakable scent —stale, sharp, and wrong. Damien has been here. I know it.

I leave the hat where it is and quietly return to Ollie without saying a word. He doesn't seem to notice the hat or anything unusual. We begin heading back toward the church to meet up with the others when Raquel rushes up behind me.

"Did you see that hat appear on the statue?" she whispers.

Ollie hears her, turns back, and does a double-take. I see it in his face— he recognizes it.

The rest of the group soon joins us, and we start walking back toward Red Mountain. I keep quiet. Ollie walks beside me and eventually breaks the silence.

"Want to see a mining shaft with a cart?" he asks.

I nod. "Sure."

I know it's his way of offering something in light of what just happened—something connected to the hat, even if I don't fully understand it yet.

Ollie then turns to the group. "Would anyone want to ride the pack mules when we get back?"

Raquel's face lights up with excitement. "Yes, definitely!"

"I can bring Octavius and Ava too," I add.

Before we can plan further, Fleur pauses mid-step. "Would anyone care for tea and pastries at the restaurant?"

We all agree without hesitation. It's a perfect way to wind down. We sit together, sipping tea, enjoying the pastries, and chatting as we watch people go by. The afternoon is calm. There's no sign of the Others today, which strikes me as strange. If they were planning something, Sunday would be the day to do it, when the town is quiet and most people are at home or in church.

Ollie catches me glancing down the road toward the Red Rock Mine. He leans closer and speaks just loud enough for me to hear.

"We could use dynamite to close the mine."

I look at him, surprised by how calmly he says it.

"There's no heavy equipment in this time period to reopen it," he explains. "It won't stop them forever, but it'll slow them down."

I nod, understanding. Ollie is just as committed to stopping the Others as I am.

On the way back, I ask Ollie, "Can we stop by the Red Rock Mine?"

He nods. "Yeah, let's check it out."

We let the rest of the group go ahead without us. Raquel insists on staying, and surprisingly, Louis does too.

When we reach the mine, it looks deserted. A wide cave entrance opens up before us, with rusted tracks leading into the darkness. Wooden beams line the walls for support, but I hesitate at the edge. Something about going in doesn't feel right.

"I don't want to go inside," I admit. "What if it collapses while we're in there?"

We all linger at the entrance, unsure.

Suddenly, in the distance, I spot two figures approaching—Leon and Wendell.

"They're coming," I whisper.

Ollie sees them too. "Where should we hide?"

"Where should we hide?" Raquel and Louis echo

We all scramble, jumping into a few of the mine carts parked out front. Crouched low, we peer out as Leon and Wendell come closer.

They stop just outside the mine. Wendell begins speaking.

"We'll extract the mineral from here. It's rare, but essential. It's what powers the Ether devices," he says. "That's why it's kept secret. Most people don't even know it exists."

Leon crosses his arms. "What's the name of it?"

Wendell chuckles. "Damien calls it Ether. Like the phrase, 'into the ether'—because that's what it looks like when people vanish using the device. They just disappear."

Leon nods. "Don't worry. The crew can start digging on Wednesday. We've got three months, covered by Damien's payment to the mine."

"Sounds good," Wendell replies, shaking his hand. "There are only a few prototype devices right now. Maybe five at most."

They walk off toward the office, still talking.

I stay quiet, stunned. So Leon is involved after all. No wonder people are willing to kill for these devices—we have two of the five.

As we climb out of the carts, I turn to Ollie. "I need tea. Or anything with caffeine and chocolate. That was a lot to process."

"There's just cornstarch cake at the house," Ollie says.

I shake my head. "It's fine. Let's go back to Red Mountain. It's probably safer anyway, especially with the Others around."

"Maybe Fleur has something to go with tea," he says. "I'll ask if there's any chocolate pudding or walnut cake."

"Please do," I say.

We begin walking back slowly toward the office at Red Mountain, all of us deep in thought. At least now we know what the Others are after—more Ether devices.

Ollie quietly offers me his arm, and I take it. We walk together, close, as the sun begins to dip lower behind the hills.

CHAPTER 17

When we arrive back at the house, Ollie heads straight to the kitchen to see what might be available for a snack. He returns with good news—Fleur had baked a fresh chocolate cake for dessert. She doesn't mind us having some now, along with tea.

Everyone takes a generous slice of cake, enjoying it with either milk or hot tea. The rich, chocolate flavor is just what I needed.

As we relax, Ollie says, "We could take the pack mules up to the top of the mountain before dinner if anyone wants to."

Fleur raises a hand. "Maybe tomorrow. That ride takes a few hours up and back."

I nod and turn to Fleur and Benjamin. "Your church in town is beautiful. It's one of the most unique I've ever seen."

Benjamin gives a small smile. "It's built over part of the Red Rock Mine. A section collapsed a few years back—right under the church. It's caused some foundation issues."

I frown. "I hope they fix it. It would be a shame to lose such a lovely place."

He nods. "I hope so, too."

Just then, Lydia walks in. "That's where I was married," she says softly.

I glance at her. "I bet it was a beautiful wedding."

"It was," she says, smiling faintly. "An evening service with the sanctuary lit entirely by candles."

Raquel lights up. "That sounds so romantic. A candlelit wedding under the stars."

Not long after, dinner is served. We have beef pot roast with potatoes and carrots—hearty and delicious. As I eat, my thoughts begin to wander. I wonder if Damien ever came back for his hat. Or if someone else took it. It's probably silly to dwell on, but I know he left it there on purpose. He wanted me to know he'd been close.

After dinner, Ollie offers to take us to the Red Mountain Mine. We follow him through the office and out toward the center of the mountain. There's a small shaft opening, partially boarded up, with old mine cart tracks leading inside.

Ollie removes a few loose boards.

"I'll go first," Louis says, stepping inside with a flashlight.

Anslow follows, then Raquel. I stay back for a moment, watching the area. A few figures stand off in the distance, just watching us.

Ollie sees me scanning the horizon. "People are always spying on this mountain," he says.

We step into the shaft together. The tunnel is quiet, the air cooler. Louis holds the flashlight up, casting shadows along the corridor. Just a few steps inside sits an old mine cart. Despite its age, it still looks solid.

As we walk farther into the mine, Louis starts to talk.

"You know, back in pioneer times, miners used to bring canaries with them," he says. "The birds were used to detect poisonous gas. If the canary died, it meant there was toxic gas in the air."

Ollie glances at him. "This mine doesn't go that far," he says. "We're almost at the end."

He's not exaggerating. We pass another mine cart, then come to a stop in front of a wall of packed dirt. The track clearly used to continue beyond this point, but now it's sealed. It appears that the tunnel was either backfilled intentionally or collapsed and subsequently blocked off.

I crouch and touch the ground. The dirt feels soft under my fingers, and the air smells musty—like old, damp earth. There's an odd drop in the ground right where the tunnel ends, like something deeper lies beneath.

I look over at Ollie. "What did they mine here? Was it iron ore or something else?"

He shakes his head. "Not sure. Probably something valuable. Or at least people believed it was. That's why everyone's so obsessed with the legends about this place."

The others begin to turn back toward the entrance. As I step to follow, something shiny on the ground catches my eye. I bend down and pick it up. It looks like a small gold nugget. It could be pyrite—fool's gold—or maybe someone placed it here on purpose. Still, it makes me wonder if there's some truth to the town's stories. Maybe gold was found here, once. Maybe Benjamin doesn't even know. It's possible the mining company took whatever was valuable and claimed there was nothing left.

I slip the nugget into the pocket of my dress.

Then I notice something else—something unusual just a few steps away. It's a black crystal with translucent royal blue and gold flecks inside. I hold it up, turning it in the light. As I watch, it shifts in color from black to smoky gray, still threaded with those sparkling specs.

I've never seen anything like it. Could this be the mineral the Others call Ether?

If they needed a color to symbolize vanishing, black would be the perfect choice.

I tuck the crystal into my pocket and head toward the entrance. The rest of the group is waiting. Louis spots me and raises an eyebrow.

"You took your time," he says, a little annoyed.

I smile faintly but say nothing.

I decide not to tell anyone about what I found. Not yet. If I tell anyone, it'll be Ollie. I know there's something hidden here at Red Mountain. I don't know if it's all been mined out or deliberately covered up—but I do know one thing: I'm going to find out the truth.

That evening, I chose to go with Ollie to the church for Bible study. The rest of the group stays back at Red Mountain to rest before tomorrow's ride up the mountain. It sounds like fun, and I'm looking forward to it.

When we arrive at the church, the first thing I do is glance over to where Damien's hat had been placed on the statue. It's gone now. That answers that question. I say nothing as we walk inside.

The next morning, we eat breakfast and prepare for the trip up the mountain. Ollie brings out blankets and saddles, setting them up carefully. He calls for the pack mules, and they come trotting over, ready for the journey. I carry my purse with Octavius and Ava inside, but I decide to leave Oscar at the house for this one.

Ollie fastens the saddles, and we all mount up. I've never ridden a horse —or anything, for that matter—and Ollie has to help me up. I'm surprised by how high off the ground it feels once I'm on the mule's back.

The mules form a single-file line, moving steadily along the side of the mountain. We loop around the back, where an old barn stands nestled against the hill. Octavius and Ava each ride in the side pockets of the saddle. Octavius is on the right, Ava on the left. They're both wide-eyed, watching everything as we climb. It's Octavius's first time riding, and I can tell he's enjoying it.

As we approach the barn, Ollie dismounts and walks ahead to open the doors. Anslow frowns. "How are we getting up the mountain by going into a barn?"

Ollie grins. He walks over and slaps Anslow's mule on the rear. The mule jolts forward, carrying a startled Anslow straight into the barn.

The rest of the mules follow, and I stop to wait for Ollie as he closes the barn doors behind us. As I ride through, the barn interior shimmers and fades—revealing a narrow, inclined corridor carved into the mountain itself.

It's a natural path that winds upward like a switchback road, hidden from the outside world. The illusion of the barn was a hologram.

I glance up the steep incline and grip the saddle tighter. Heights aren't my favorite, and now that I can see just how high we'll be climbing, I begin to wonder how long this will take.

The heat is starting to settle in, too. I glance down at the mule beneath me and feel a pang of sympathy.

"Poor thing," I murmur. "It must be sweltering under this saddle and blanket."

Still, we continue upward, slowly but steadily, toward the summit. I glance back at Ollie, who smiles at me. Ahead of us, I see Raquel talking with Louis while Anslow's mule hurries ahead, eager to reach the top.

As I round the first corner and continue the ascent, I notice how the terrain changes. We're now on the side of the hill, and the higher we climb, the more jagged and solid the mountain becomes. There are no longer natural paths, just rough, uneven ridges shaped by time. I can't imagine anyone willingly climbing past this natural switchback. A strange feeling creeps in—the sense of being watched. I glance around, scanning the mountain, but see no one except the group.

After a while, Ollie asks, "Want to take a break and drink some water?"

We all agree. It's a good moment to stop and catch our breath. I ask him, "Where do the mules get water?"

He points to a nearby water pump and walks over to fill a bucket. The mules move in and drink at their own pace.

Louis empties his canteen and refills it at the pump. I'm just as thirsty and take a few long sips. Ollie glances around at us.

"There's plenty more water at the top," he says.

We climb back onto the mules and continue upward. The only sound now is the steady rhythm of hooves against rock. Everyone has gone quiet, lost in their own thoughts. I glance back at Ollie again. He's looking up at the towering mountain walls lining our path.

At last, we begin to near the summit—at least the summit of this side of the mountain. The actual peak of Red Mountain rises much higher still, with no flat ground in sight. I feel relieved to be almost there. The wind picks up, stronger now that we're exposed. With the natural walls on either side of the trail, we haven't had many chances to look out over the edge during the climb.

Just ahead, I see the path level off. Anslow's mule trots over the last rise and disappears onto the summit. Raquel gasps.

I begin to wonder what she saw.

Ava and Octavius cheer with excitement as they reach the top. I follow close behind. As I crest the incline, the view opens up, and what I see takes my breath away. It's an oasis.

At the center is a calm pond, bordered by lush gardens and fruit trees. A small cabin sits nearby, complete with a wooden deck and patio furniture. It feels like something out of a dream.

I ask Ollie about the cabin.

"It's for when Fleur and Benjamin don't feel like coming down," he says. "Sometimes they stay up here and work on the crops. There's a hologram that covers this whole area, so even if someone flew over in a hot air balloon, all they'd see is a blank mountain top."

WE BEGIN LOOKING around as we dismount the mules. There are several raised garden beds arranged in long rows, bursting with leafy greens, potatoes, grapes, and even cotton. Ollie mentions they use the cotton to make their own fabrics. The wood paneling on each bed is painted in bright colors—turquoise, orange, red, and yellow—giving the area a cheerful, handmade charm. The cabin itself is painted a minty green shade that stands out against the earthy mountain surroundings.

"If anyone needs water, a snack, or the restroom, the cabin's open," Ollie offers.

I'm tempted to see the inside of the cabin, but something at the far edge of the summit catches my eye. I walk toward a natural rock wall and notice a wooden door tucked into it. Curious, I approach and gently push it. It creaks open slowly.

What I see inside takes my breath away.

It's a large room carved into the mountain, filled with gold bars stacked in high rows. In the center sits a desk surrounded by a few sofas and a small coffee table. Off to one side is a treasure chest, smaller but unmistakably ornate. Light filters in from above through natural openings in the rock ceiling, casting soft beams across the golden surfaces. Toward the back, I spot another door. It appears the space extends deeper.

I step back, carefully closing the door behind me. No one noticed where I went, and I decided not to mention it—at least not yet.

I head toward the cabin, hoping for a cup of tea and something sweet. Up close, the cabin reminds me so much of the one near Rocky Creek, the first place I stayed when I met Ollie at his cattle ranch. There's something comforting in that familiarity.

The main difference is that the kitchenette is in the same spot as the fireplace. This kitchen, though, is modern. The rest of the house looks the same, except now there's a modern restroom up in the loft.

I sit at the kitchen table drinking tea with Raquel. We're talking about how Ollie let her and Anslow pick some dates and grapes. There's nothing sweet at the cabin except the fruit. As she talks about her morning, I find myself thinking back to everything I saw in the room not long ago.

"Ava and Octavius have been having so much fun," Raquel says. "They've been climbing the fruit trees and helping toss dates down into a basket."

After we finish our tea, we head outside and see Ava and Octavius splashing around the edge of the pond. I glance around the lovely garden, but my eyes drift toward the door at the end of the summit. It's ajar now. I wonder who's there. Has someone from the group gone in and seen what's inside?

I walk over quietly, trying not to draw attention. Standing by the door, I listen. I could swear I hear Ollie whispering to someone. My chest tightens. I don't want to find out he's with the bad guys, not after everything we've been through.

I nudge the door open a bit more and try to peek inside. Ollie's back is to me, blocking whoever he's talking to. Could it be Lydia? That would make sense.

I wait, hoping he'll shift enough for me to see. But then the door lets out a squeak, and Ollie turns around. His eyes widen. He looks startled. Then Damien stands up.

The sight hits me hard. I feel betrayed. Hurt. Without thinking, I turn and start running back toward the garden.

"Wait!" Ollie calls after me. "I can explain."

I pause, just barely. Then, out of the corner of my eye, I see Benjamin approaching the room. I feel ambushed. Should I use one of the Ether devices now?

Before I can speak, Damien starts talking. Benjamin steps inside and cuts him off.

"Ollie, is everything alright? I saw the security breach on the system and came as fast as I could."

But where did Benjamin even come from?

Benjamin looks at me and says, "It probably isn't my place to say this, but Damien is Ollie's dad."

I stare at him, stunned. He continues, "Damien married Lydia and had two sons. Both were born without the mutations. Ollie hadn't even been born yet in 1855, but the timeline is... complicated. The older version of Lydia is the Lydia from 1855. That's why Ollie wanted to avoid seeing her—so he wouldn't risk any time continuum disturbances."

Time continuum disturbances are the only things that have happened with the Ether device. I turn to Ollie.

"Why didn't you tell me Damien is your dad?"

He hesitates. "I was afraid to. I don't support what the others are doing with the Ether devices, but... he's still my dad. I didn't want to lose you, so I just stayed quiet."

He pauses, then adds, "Honestly, having Damien as a father is a lot, even for me. I can't imagine how it would be for you."

I shift the subject. "What about the mine and the gold?"

Benjamin nods. "When I bought the mine, it was worthless. I found out why pretty quickly. The entire thing, which ran deep under Red Mountain, had collapsed. We didn't bother digging it out. Instead, we moved the operation to another location that had potential for Ether minerals."

He folds his arms. "Nobody cared about anything but Ether. But after living here for a while, we found chambers near the center of the mountain —and those held gold."

"Did Damien know?" I ask.

Benjamin shakes his head. "Not until today. And I don't think he'll try to take it, considering it's his son's inheritance."

I take a breath. "And the cattle ranch?"

"That was funded by Fleur's cookbooks, just like we said. We lived in Rocky Creek for a while, where Lydia grew up and built the home that became the orphanage. After Lydia married Damien, we moved out here to get away from it all."

I don't know what to think. But we can't stay hidden for long—not after finding out the Others live underground in massive cities, the same way you live in your above-ground dome cities.

Lydia, being married to Damien, gains access to her own Ether device. That's how our home here ends up decorated in different time periods.

I glance at the coffee table. "What's in the treasure chest?" I ask.

Benjamin walks over and picks it up. "This," he says, "is my real treasure."

He opens the chest slowly and holds it up. Inside is a Bible.

"This is all you need to be the wealthiest man in the world," he says, his voice steady.

He sets the chest back down. We all stare at one another in silence for a moment, unsure what to say.

CHAPTER 18

$\mathcal{I}$ walk out to the garden to process everything I've just heard. After a while, I head back to the cabin for more tea. I sit alone, thinking.

I don't know why Ollie didn't tell me. Then again, it makes sense. From the very beginning, he never seemed surprised—never even flinched when someone stepped out of a time portal. That kind of automatic acceptance is what made me feel safe with him. I could trust him because he didn't judge me for being different or for not fitting into the social norms and customs of life in 1880.

Right now, I miss Oscar. Hugging him, watching him play—it brings me comfort. I start to wonder how all of this will unfold. How will Ollie react, knowing that I know? And how will I react to him, now that I do?

Raquel comes in after a while. "We're heading back down the mountain soon," she says gently.

"I'll be out shortly," I tell her, glancing at my cup. "Just want to finish my tea."

She looks at me for a moment. "What's wrong?"

"I got some bad news," I say quietly. "I just need a little time to myself."

She seems surprised but smiles. "Alright. I'll be out in the garden when you're ready."

She leaves, and I feel a little bad for not being more social. I bow my head and pray, asking the Lord for guidance. When I finish my tea, I step outside and see everyone gathering around the mules. Octavius and Ava are already seated, looking at me as if waiting for me to join the group. Ollie stands nearby with Anslow and Louis.

I step forward, putting on a smile, even if it's not quite real. I walk over to the mule I rode up with as everyone begins to mount theirs for the trip back down.

As we start down the trail, Ava turns to me. "I fed the mules leafy green vegetables," she says proudly.

Ollie rides behind me again, the last one to descend. I glance over my shoulder and meet his eyes. He smiles at me, and I feel better. There's a kind of relief in knowing he hasn't changed toward me, even now that I know his secret.

I wonder if Vicki knows, too. Maybe I'll never find out.

The way down the mountain is much faster than the climb up. Anslow and Louis are having fun as the mules breeze along the trail, descending with ease. I keep praying silently, asking for guidance in all of this.

As we reach the bottom, we exit the barn and dismount. The mules wander off in search of pasture. I feel relieved to be back down Red Mountain. My thoughts drift to Damien and the Others who live underground. I wonder if the mine collapse here at Red Mine was intentional—meant to stop the Others from gaining access to the Ether mineral.

Ollie comes over and starts making small talk.

"So," he says, "what did you think about going up the mountain today?"

"I liked it," I reply. "Though I'm not a fan of heights."

Ava and Octavius are running around nearby, marveling at the desert. I reach into my pocket and pull out the gold nugget and the small, faintly translucent crystal I found yesterday in the Red Mountain mine. I hand them to Ollie.

"I think this crystal must be the Ether mineral," I say. "I've never seen anything like it."

Ollie's eyes widen. "I was going to tell you," he blurts out. "About my parents, and the Ether devices. I just... wanted to wait until we knew each other better. I wasn't sure if you'd still want to associate with me."

I look him in the eye. "I do. I want you to feel like you don't have to hide anything from me."

He nods, visibly relieved. "I won't. No more secrets. I promise."

Then he lowers his voice. "I'm planning to collapse the mine in town tomorrow. Using dynamite."

I stare at him. "Isn't that dangerous? And... why? Especially considering your dad is an Other?"

"I love my dad," Ollie says. "But that doesn't mean I agree with what he does. Just because someone's your parent doesn't mean you have to follow in their footsteps."

Ollie looks at the Ether mineral in his hand. "We need to be careful with this," he says. "A piece this small could get someone killed if the Others find out."

He reaches out to hand me back the gold nugget, but I shake my head. "Keep it," I tell him. "It's the least I can do for your kindness."

Ollie looks at me, his expression softening. "I was already ready to help you when I got on that train with you in Rocky Creek."

I smile, but still insist. "Then let it be a thank-you."

We walk back around to the office entrance to head inside. Ava and Octavius run along beside us, their steps light and quick. Even with their chatter, I still feel that strange sense of being watched. I glance around, but nothing seems out of place.

Once we're inside, Benjamin walks up and quietly asks to speak with Ollie. My nerves flicker. I step aside to give them privacy, though I stay within view. I watch them talk for a few minutes. Then Benjamin walks over to the bookshelf, picks up a small treasure chest, and hands it to Ollie. He opens it and pulls out a gold-colored Bible, elegant and beautifully made. Benjamin wraps Ollie in a hug, and Ollie thanks him softly.

Ollie comes over to show me the Bible. I flip through the pages and notice that at the beginning of every book, there's an illustration. Each one is detailed and delicate, suggesting it must have taken a long time to create.

Just then, Fleur calls us for supper. Ollie carefully places the Bible back into the case.

After supper, Ollie tells me, "I'm going into town tomorrow to run an errand. After that, I'm starting the operation at the Red Rock Mine."

Louis, who's nearby, hears and asks, "What's Operation Red Rock Mine?"

Ollie turns to him. "It's our next move. You'll see."

Louis nods slowly. "Count me in."

Anslow, listening from across the room, chimes in too. "I'm in."

It's official—we're meeting Ollie tomorrow morning at the mine in town.

Before heading off for the night, Ollie turns to Louis and Anslow. "Before I leave tomorrow, I'll pack one of the mules. The dynamite will be hidden in the saddle pouches."

Louis and Anslow exchange a glance and grin, clearly excited about the plan. I watch Ollie for a moment as he reaches into his pocket, pulls out the Ether mineral, and places it gently in the treasure chest alongside the Bible. He catches me watching him.

"I'll ask Benjamin later to lock it in his safe," he says.

Then, lowering his voice, he adds, "Don't tell the others about the Ether mineral just yet. It's too dangerous. They don't need to know—not right now."

I smile at Ollie and nod in agreement. That evening, he plays the piano while we enjoy dessert in the living room. Fleur serves chocolate pudding and the leftover chocolate cake from yesterday, along with tea. Ollie seems more relaxed, more like himself. I can see the relief on his face—he knows I understand the truth now, and nothing has changed between us.

I glance at Lydia and wonder what she ever saw in Damien, considering his obsession with world domination. She seems like the embodiment of the wild west—untamed, bold, and unconcerned with the social norms of the East. She wears pants, rides horses bareback if needed, and holds herself with a freedom few possess.

Watching Ollie tonight, I realize how much of him is shaped by those around him. His confidence and boldness come from Lydia. His generosity is clearly Benjamin's. From Fleur, he gets his deep compassion. But the way he makes me feel safe—that's entirely his own. That's just Ollie.

The next morning, Fleur makes pancakes again, this time with pecans and maple syrup. The room is full of cheerful conversation until Ollie reminds everyone, "Don't forget about Operation Red Rock Mine."

He turns to Louis and Anslow. "I'll get the pack mule ready. All you need to do is get it into town quietly and wait for me to come back to the mine."

After finishing the work in the barn and handing the mule off to Louis, Ollie seems content. He heads into town on foot. Anslow lingers behind and looks uneasy.

"I don't know about this," he says. "I'm kind of afraid of dynamite. What if something goes wrong?"

Louis, full of confidence, grins and flexes. "Don't worry. I've got it covered."

Raquel walks over just in time to see the mule and hear about the plan. Louis straightens up even more.

Curious, I quietly follow Ollie from a distance. He walks to a small shop, reaches into his pocket, and pulls out the gold nugget from yesterday. He's selling it. After a while, he comes out and heads to a jewelry store.

He's inside for quite some time. I don't recall him mentioning the need to visit a jewelry store. Then it hits me—maybe he's having his pocket watch repaired.

But when he leaves, he's carrying a small gift box, which he slips into his coat pocket. So it's not a repair. He bought something. Maybe a new pocket watch?

I smirk a little. *Time will tell*, I think, and quietly laugh to myself.

Realizing I've been following him too closely, I duck into a storefront and try to look like I'm just window shopping. As he walks by, he notices me.

"You spying on me?" he teases.

I start to answer, but he smiles. "Come on. Join me for tea at the restaurant."

I blink in surprise. "Aren't you supposed to be blowing up a mine?"

He grins. "It can wait for tea."

"After blowing up the mine, we can come back and have tea and cake," I say with a smile.

Ollie nods. "Sounds like a plan."

We head over to the mine, where everyone is already gathered around the mule. Ollie walks over, carefully removes the dynamite, and heads into the mine. Louis turns on a flashlight, and the two of them walk ahead, searching for the right spot to place the charges. After a few minutes of quiet discussion, they agree on a section and begin setting it up.

Ollie looks back at the rest of us. "Alright, everyone out. I'll light the fuses."

It's dark inside the mine, and only Louis has a flashlight. He holds it steady so Ollie can see as he lights the fuses. Once they're lit, we all take off running as fast as we can with the limited light we have. Ollie had said earlier that bringing too many flashlights might draw attention, since their brightness is more noticeable than lanterns.

We sprint out of the mine, heading toward Red Mountain. The mule follows without needing much encouragement. Ollie runs beside me and takes my arm just as we hear the explosion behind us. The ground shakes beneath our feet. We stop and turn around.

A huge cloud of smoke and dust shoots up from the mine shaft. A massive heap of rock and dirt completely blocks the mine entrance. It's clear the collapse is total.

We stand there for a few moments, catching our breath. "That'll slow them down," Ollie says quietly.

Everyone knows people will be returning to the area by Wednesday. We're likely to find out by tomorrow how the Others react to what's happened.

We make our way to the restaurant for tea and walnut cake. As we sit, more and more people gather near the mine, clearly realizing something has gone wrong. I have a feeling we won't have to wait until tomorrow to get a response from the Others.

Ollie keeps an eye on the growing crowd. "Let's eat quickly and head back to Red Mountain," he says.

By the time we pass the mine again, the pack mule has already returned home. A few townspeople call out to us, waving us over to take a look.

"Come see what happened!" someone shouts.

We try to act surprised, careful not to say anything false. Ollie responds, "We've got to get back to Red Mountain," and keeps walking.

I glance back one last time. *What if someone else had collapsed Red Mountain Mine the same way Ollie just did, and for the same reason?*

Once we're back inside, we decide to stay here for a while and have a group meeting to figure out what to do next.

"Let's go back to the orphanage," I suggest, "check on Vicki, and return Raquel. Then we can return to my time and take Louis home."

I turn to Anslow. "You can stay in 1855 or return to 1880—it's up to you."

He doesn't answer right away. He nods slightly, a disappointed look on his face, no matter which option is offered.

Ollie speaks up. "Let's sleep on it," he says. "We're safe here. Rushing into a decision might not be the wisest choice after everything that happened today."

I agree. "You're right. We'll think about it and decide tomorrow."

Still, I can't help but feel sorry for Anslow. He doesn't seem to have anyone beyond us. And though we've all grown close, he still avoids talking about what happened to him.

Later, I go to the guest room and begin packing, just in case we leave in the morning. Ollie stops by and tells Raquel and me, "Lydia says you can keep the dresses. She knows you lost your luggage."

I smile. "That's really kind of her. I'm glad I met your mom and got to know your grandparents. They've been so hospitable."

But I can tell everyone is feeling torn. No one seems eager to return to their old lives. Instead, we're all thinking about staying together in another time. Even at supper, the mood is quiet and unsure.

I feel a twinge of guilt for pushing the idea of leaving so soon. Still, I believe it's right to at least try to return everyone to where they came from.

Later that evening, I sit with Oscar. He's happy here. Fleur sneaks him treats and lets him play with yarn balls. He purrs and curls up next to me.

From the living room, I hear raised voices. I walk toward the sound and see Benjamin holding a letter, visibly upset. Ollie is beside him.

"It says, 'We acknowledge it was you,'" Benjamin tells him. "What happened?"

Ollie explains quietly. "It was my plan. Operation Red Rock Mine."

Benjamin listens carefully. He looks surprised, but not entirely shocked.

"I understand why you did it," he says at last. "But you've stirred something. You're playing a dangerous game with the Others."

He pauses, then adds, "You should go back to 1880. At least for a little while."

The mood in the room shifts. Everyone goes quiet. The air feels heavy, full of unspoken disappointment.

I glance at Ollie, who looks back at me with a soft sigh.

"Hey," I say gently, trying to lift the mood. "This doesn't have to be permanent. We can always come back later."

That seems to help. Faces brighten just a little, and the heaviness starts to lift.

We all begin to prepare, knowing tomorrow morning will be our last pancake breakfast here—for now.

No one feels like playing the piano or celebrating. Instead, the group gathers for Bible study and prayer. Afterward, we all bed head. But I can't sleep. I lie there, my thoughts filled with Ollie and what might happen if we ever got separated. I'm also sad thinking about saying goodbye to Raquel— and even Anslow. Louis is returning to a life defined by his job, and I'm unsure where I fit into it.

I pray quietly, asking God for guidance, and somewhere in the middle of my thoughts, I begin to drift off.

The next morning, Fleur makes pecan pancakes and tea. The room is quiet as we eat, everyone savoring each bite. Oscar walks lazily around the house before curling up to nap on one of the sofas. After breakfast, we begin packing. I gently place Oscar back into the picnic basket and check to make sure Ava and Octavius are tucked safely in my purse.

We say our goodbyes to the Loughrys. Fleur hugs me tightly.

"I'm so pleased to have met you," she says with warmth in her voice.

"Thank you," I whisper back. "You've made this feel like home."

Soon, we gather in the round cave room where the Ether device will activate. I turn to Anslow one last time.

"Are you sure you don't want to stay in 1855?"

He shakes his head. "No. I want to help fix the time continuum—for you."

I smile, touched. "That's one of the nicest things anyone's ever said to me."

I pull out the Ether device and take a deep breath, double-checking that

Ava and Octavius are secure in my purse and Oscar is safe in the basket. I wave goodbye to Fleur and Benjamin.

The Ether device hums to life. Energy pulses through it as the stale, heavy air begins to swirl around us. Everyone clings to me tightly as the current builds.

In the next instant, we find ourselves sprawled on the ground in front of the orphanage.

I don't feel any rush to stand up. The moment feels too heavy. But then I hear a voice—familiar and frantic—calling out.

I look up and see Vicki running toward us at full speed, tears streaming down her face. She reaches Raquel first, wrapping her in a fierce hug, then comes to me, then to Ollie. Anslow opens his arms for a hug, but Vicki pauses, looking him over.

"Who are you?" she asks.

Louis stands a bit behind us, calmly surveying the area. Vicki pulls away slightly, her expression turning serious.

"I have bad news," she says, and we all turn to her, bracing ourselves for what's coming next.

CHAPTER 19

*V*icki looks down, her expression heavy. "The Others are trying to get the orphanage shut down," she says quietly.

She explains that Harvey, Ollie's brother, has given them a two-month notice to vacate the house. At least, that's what the letter says. But Vicki isn't convinced.

"I don't even know if the letter is really from Harvey," she adds. "It doesn't sound like him. He's never cared much about the orphanage either way."

Ollie speaks up. "I'll go to Chapel Hill today and talk to Harvey myself."

As soon as he says it, I feel uneasy. Something about Ollie going to see his brother fills me with dread. Vicki looks worried, too. This isn't easy for Ollie. He cares about the orphanage just as deeply as she does.

Louis and Anslow stand nearby, clearly unaware of what's going on. I can't blame them; they haven't been here long. But I don't feel like explaining it all right now.

Vicki invites everyone inside for tea and chocolate cake. I smile. "Vicki, you've read my mind."

As we settle inside, Anslow begins looking around the house and pointing out little repairs he could make—things to fix or paint. Vicki listens, but I can tell she's not really hearing him. Her thoughts are elsewhere, focused entirely on saving the orphanage.

Ollie leans toward me and asks, "Would you like to go to dinner with me in town later?"

I nod. "I'd love to."

He plans to visit Harvey after dinner. I think it's a good idea for us to talk things through before he goes.

Pricella comes down the stairs, and Vicki offers her tea and cake too. As they sit together, Vicki gently asks, "What would you do if we had to move out?"

Pricella sighs. "I'd either move in with my sister, but she's all the way across the country. The problem has always been the train fare. My daughter and I couldn't afford it."

Ollie replies without hesitation. "I can help with tickets—for both of you."

Vicki gives a soft smile. "Well, that's three people taken care of. Now I just have to figure out what to do with the other five children."

Pricella hesitates, then adds, "I've actually been thinking about adopting the two girls. There's been a marriage proposal I've been praying about."

She looks a little embarrassed but continues. "He's an attorney. He doesn't have children, which isn't surprising given he's marrying later in life. He said he's open to adoption. Maybe... maybe this is the answer I've been waiting for."

Vicki listens quietly, absorbing every word.

Vicki smiles gently at Pricella. "I'm happy for you. I hope he'll be a good husband—and a good father to your children."

Pricella nods. "I'll make a decision soon. I'm still praying about it."

Ollie turns to her. "If you do decide to go back east, let me know. I'll help with the arrangements."

Pricella gives him a warm smile. "Thank you, Ollie."

Raquel remains quiet through most of the conversation, and I understand why. She's thinking about Frank.

After a pause, she speaks. "Vicki, have you seen Frank lately?"

Vicki shakes her head. "I haven't. And honestly, I hope he stays gone."

Raquel sighs. "He still owes me money, but I'd rather just let it go. I want to move on with my life. I don't ever want to see him again."

Vicki places a comforting hand on her arm. "Your father isn't the one who defines who you are. God is. Whether he stayed or left doesn't change that. You're a daughter of God, Raquel."

She continues, her voice calm and sure. "When we obey God, we walk in His power. He works all things for the good of those who love Him. And those who love Him, obey Him."

Raquel smiles and sips her tea, the words settling in.

Later, Ollie and I get ready to go into town for dinner. Vicki and the others look a little surprised, but I'm glad he asked. We need time to talk—just the two of us. In truth, I trust Ollie more than I trust anyone else right now.

As we walk past the front of the orphanage, Ollie suddenly stops and turns to face me. Then he gets down on one knee and opens a small jewelry box. Inside is a beautiful sapphire ring set in silver.

"I almost got a pearl ring," he says, "but then I remembered your favorite color is blue."

I gasp and pick up the ring, stunned.

Ollie looks up at me. "Will you marry me?"

"Yes!" I say, without hesitation.

We hug tightly. When I finally open my eyes, I notice something. The whole group is standing outside, watching us.

Ollie follows my gaze and turns around. Vicki gives us a knowing smile. "I had a feeling something was going on," she says.

Everyone claps. Raquel runs up, beaming. "When's the wedding? I want to know everything!"

Ollie takes the ring from me and gently slides it onto my finger. It's almost a perfect fit.

"If you need it adjusted, we can get it resized," he says.

Then he adds softly, "I wanted to propose here—right where I first saw you. Ever since that day, I've just wanted to be around you. I couldn't explain it. I just knew I wanted to be near you."

Ollie suggests, "Why don't we all go out to eat at the Corner Café to celebrate?"

It's a great idea, and everyone agrees as we begin walking toward town. As we walk, I glance down at my ring. It looks beautiful, catching the light just right. I catch Ollie looking at me, and he smiles when he sees me admiring it.

I hardly notice the heat this time. As we get closer to town, I glance over at Precilla and wonder aloud, "Where are all the children today?"

"They've gone into town to try and raise money," Vicki says. "Doing odd jobs wherever they can. If the orphanage closes, every bit helps."

Precilla nods. "I've been taking on seamstress work and baking from the garden—pies, preserves, anything we can sell. I've even started making aprons and tablecloths."

"I wish the kids could join us for dinner," I say. "Maybe afterward we can give them a little spending money, let them pick out candy from the general store."

"I think they'd like that," Vicki replies softly.

When we arrive at the Corner Café, we sit down and the waitress brings us menus. Vicki and Precilla quietly read theirs, but I can tell their minds are elsewhere. They look tired, heavy with worry. Still, I believe in my heart that God will help them. He always makes a way.

After dinner, we gather outside, each of us silently thinking about what to do next. I glance toward the train station and see Philip selling newspapers. He's a little dirty, with patches on his pants, but he's laughing and talking with another boy. They look happy in that moment. Philip may understand he needs to earn money, but he doesn't grasp what he's missing out on.

Louis stands next to me, watching without knowing who he's looking at.

"That boy," I whisper, "he's your ancestor."

Louis doesn't respond. He's too busy laughing with Anslow. Philip walks by and offers him a paper.

"Paper, sir? Two cents."

Louis stops. "Sure," he says, and turns to Ollie. "You got any change?"

Ollie hands him a coin, and Louis buys the paper, clearly proud of himself. He has no idea what that small exchange truly means.

Ollie excuses himself to buy a train ticket while the rest of us wait nearby. As we stand there, Raquel turns to me with a bright smile.

"I'm happy for you again," she says. "Soon you'll be Mrs. Desiree Newton."

I pause for a second and shake my head. "No, I'll be Desiree Loughry."

Vicki chimes in gently, "Actually, Loughry is his mother's maiden name. Newton is his father's last name."

I glance down at the newspaper Philip had handed us earlier. The date catches my eye—June 18th, 1880. Something about it feels so familiar, but I can't quite place it. A strange feeling of dread and panic creeps over me, and I have no idea why.

"Ollie Newton... Rocky Creek, Arizona..." I whisper to myself, my mind scrambling. "Why does that sound so important?"

Then it hits me—June 18th, 1880—the day of the shootout at Chapel Hill.

The memory rushes in. I don't remember every detail, but I know Ollie is supposed to go talk to his brother. During that meeting, they'll get into an argument with the exact rancher Harvey had issues with over missing cattle. A shootout breaks out. Ollie dies. His brother survives.

"No," I breathe out. "No, no, no."

I take off running toward the ticket window. As I scan the area, I spot Ollie standing on the platform, speaking with a man. As I approach, I catch a piece of their conversation.

"We can settle it once and for all," the man says. "You and I can go together to talk to him. I want you to know I'm not behind the missing cattle."

That has to be Harvey.

Ollie nods. "Alright. We can go. I want to discuss the orphanage with you on the way, too."

"No!" I yell, rushing up. "You can't go!"

Ollie and Harvey both turn to look at me. Harvey frowns.

"What is she going on about?" he asks, clearly annoyed.

Ollie looks confused. "Desiree, what are you talking about?"

"I remember now," I say, trying to catch my breath. "You can't go. There's going to be a shootout. You die today at Chapel Hill. Please, Ollie. Don't go."

Harvey steps back, shaking his head. "Is this some kind of joke?"

"It's not a joke," I snap. "I know how this ends."

Ollie puts a hand on my shoulder. "Come with me," he says softly. "Let's talk."

We walk away from the platform. My heart is pounding. I start telling Ollie everything I remember from the historical accounts. As I speak, I feel a sudden tug from my purse. I know it's Octavius trying to get my attention.

I tug back slightly, signaling him to wait. Not now.

Ollie watches me with a mix of concern and disbelief. "Desiree…"

"Please," I say, my voice breaking. "Don't go. Stay here. I can't lose you."

Ollie agrees not to go today to meet his brother at Chapel Hill. As we stand there, he turns to me with a serious expression.

"Do you think that's enough to change the time continuum?" he asks. Then, after a pause, "I thought you wanted to restore it… even if that meant I'd have to die."\

I shake my head. "I don't care about the time continuum right now. I care about you. I want you to be safe, Ollie. I can't imagine my life without you."

He looks at me for a moment, then nods. "Let's just go back to the orphanage and rest for the day. It won't hurt anything to wait one more day to talk to Harvey."

I smile, relieved. "If the whole Yellow Falcon Tribe avoided death on my watch, then why can't you?"

Ollie laughs softly, and we start walking back to the group.

Back at the orphanage, I help Vicki and Precilla with chores to earn a little extra money. Ollie works with Anslow and Louis out back, helping with the garden and doing repairs around the property. The day turns out to be calm and pleasant. Vicki mentions she's thinking about making fried chicken for supper.

"It sounds good," I say, wiping my hands on a towel.

"It takes time to make for so many people," Precilla says. "If we're doing it, we'd better get started soon."

Just then, we hear a knock at the door.

I go to answer it. It's Harvey.

"I'm looking for Ollie," he says.

"He's not home," I reply quickly, trying to block the doorway.

But Harvey pushes past me, followed closely by another man. "Ollie!" he calls out as he heads toward the back of the house.

They go through the kitchen and out the back door. In the yard, they find Ollie, and Harvey immediately brings up the missing cattle. Ollie tries to stay calm.

"I'm not picking sides," he says. "We can talk about it peacefully."

But the other man cuts him off. "You're a liar."

Before anyone can react, the man pulls out a gun and shoots Ollie.

I freeze in shock as I see him fall to the ground. Anslow lunges at the shooter and punches him. They fight, while Louis scrambles to get the man's gun. Harvey takes off running, leaving Ollie bleeding in the yard.

I can barely breathe. I remember from history that Ollie lived about forty-five minutes after being shot—and then he died.

I rush into the house and grab my purse.

Vicki meets me in the doorway. "What are you doing?"

"I'm getting help," I say. "The best way I know how."

I activate the Ether device using the coordinates for my house. I can feel the device pulsing, and I know it's causing Ollie pain, but we have no choice. Vicki screams as she runs toward us, but her voice fades as my bedroom begins to come into view.

I feel the pull toward the ground and stumble forward, then quickly get up and call out, "Octavius!"

He appears instantly and activates the emergency medical alarm for my address. I grab Ollie's hands and hold on tightly.

"Don't leave me," I whisper, beginning to pray.

About fifteen minutes later, someone pounds on the door. I rush to open it, and medical personnel enter quickly. One of them, a woman, sets up a device that emits a holographic image—almost transparent and floating—allowing us to see inside Ollie's body where he was shot.

Six small disks hover around him. They move smoothly, serving as advanced medical tools. I watch as two of them focus on the wound. Within minutes, the bullet is drawn out, and a fine laser begins closing the wound. On the screen, I can see how the bleeding stops and the doctor carefully navigates the disks to avoid permanent nerve or tissue damage.

About thirty minutes later, the woman turns to me.

"He's stable," she says. "In good condition. He'll need to be on antibiotics for a week, but there should be no long-term damage. We were able to repair everything."

She looks at me. "I'll need his identification. And how did he get shot?"

"He doesn't have any identification," I reply cautiously.

She studies me for a second. "Is he a Rebel?"

I hesitate. I don't answer.

The doctor gives a slight nod. "I went into medicine to help people. Even if that means overlooking a few... questionable circumstances."

She walks over to her bag and pulls out the antibiotics.

"I won't report it," she says, handing them to me. "But don't make a habit of this."

"Thank you," I say sincerely. "For your help. And for your generosity."

She checks on Ollie one last time, then leaves quietly.

Now I sit there, unsure what to do. Should we wait a while before going back, or return right away?

I decide to give Ollie his first dose of antibiotics and let him rest. As I set out some takeout, I ask, "Do you want pizza or Chinese?"

He opens his eyes and smiles faintly. "Honestly? I'm thirstier than anything."

I decided to order pizza since it's quick and easy. Ollie looks drowsy, and I know he needs to rest. I help him sit up long enough to change out of his blood-stained shirt, then guide him to the bed and gently clean the rest of the dried blood from his skin with a washcloth.

The pizza arrives, and he manages to eat a couple of slices. I hand him a glass of water, and he takes his medicine before drifting off to sleep.

Once I'm sure he's resting, I decide to return briefly to the orphanage to check on everyone and see what's happened since we left. I activate the Ether device and go back.

When I arrive, chaos greets me. The man who shot Ollie has returned—with backup. A few of them are trying to set fire to the orphanage.

I rush inside, panicked, and find Vicki and Raquel gathering what they can.

"They're trying to burn it down," Vicki says, breathless. "Just in case we can't stop them—we're grabbing anything we can save."

"Where's Oscar?" I ask. "And the kids?"

"Pricella's already gone," Vicki replies. "She left with her daughter and the two other girls from the orphanage. Said this whole thing made her realize that the marriage offer didn't sound so bad after all."

I spot Philip clinging to Vicki's side, clearly frightened. Outside, I see Anslow and Louis trying to hold the men off.

Louis shouts, "This is all happening because that guy's mad at Anslow for punching him!"

Anslow yells back, "Well, he deserved it! That's Texas justice!"

Louis fires back, "We're not in Texas!"

I turn to Vicki. "Get everyone together. Now."

Just then, Raquel runs in from the kitchen.

"I was locking the back door," she says. "Trying to keep them out."

"Come on, all of you!" I yell. "Get over here—now!"

I scoop Oscar up under my arm. The little boys scream as I activate the Ether device. They've never seen a portal before, and the sudden light terrifies them.

I didn't even check which device I grabbed.

In an instant, we're in an open field near the Rebels' settlement. The wind is calm, but the air carries tension.

I turn to Raquel.

"Find June," I say. "Tell her what happened. She'll help. She'll know what to do."

Philip stands frozen, still clutching Vicki tightly.

"It's okay," I whisper. "You're safe now."

I pull Oscar closer, then activate the Ether device again.

I'm back in my house with Ollie, who is sound asleep. I sit quietly and watch him for a while, grateful he's still here. Octavius and Ava are on their charge pads, resting peacefully. Oscar is wandering around the kitchen, poking through the pantry for a snack. I let him have some cheese and pepperoni, which seems to satisfy him.

I close my eyes and begin to pray. I thank God for saving Ollie and for protecting the others. I ask for guidance and direction—what to do next, where to go from here. I pray for the orphanage, that it might be spared and made whole again, so Vicki and the children can return to it safely.

Sleepiness begins to settle over me. Not wanting to leave Ollie's side, I decide to lie down on the floor beside the bed. If he needs anything or if the others return, I'll be nearby.

Oscar curls up next to me, warm and content, and I drift off to sleep.

CHAPTER 20

J wake up and find Ollie still sleeping soundly. I sit quietly for a moment, wondering how everyone is doing at the Rebel settlement. I look at Ollie again. I don't want to wake him. He needs the rest right now. I try to push away any thoughts about the time continuum.

Octavius and Ava stir on their charge pads and look over at me.

"How's Ollie doing?" Octavius asks.

"He's recovering," I say. "Resting well."

I start making plans to stay here for a few days while Ollie heals. After that, we can go back to the Rebel settlement to check on everyone. I think about the orphanage and what might have happened after we left. I wonder if Harvey is alright. He left Ollie there and ran instead of helping. That thought sits heavy in my chest.

Oscar trots into the room and jumps up onto the bed beside Ollie. He curls up next to him, his small body warming the space between them. I sit nearby, praying and reading the Bible. After a while, hunger creeps in. I'm trying to decide what to eat, but I don't want to leave Ollie alone for too long. If the Others show up, I need to be here.

I decide to walk to the café around the corner and get soup for Ollie. I'll find something for myself, too, and bring everything back. It's been a long time since I had an iced tea.

I grab my purse but pause—Octavius and Ava are still here, not inside it. I decide to leave them and head out quickly.

Once outside, I hurry to the café. A tiny waiter-shaped holographic device at one of the tables lights up as I approach. I browse the menu and place my order by speaking directly to it. After paying, I wait about fifteen minutes until the food is ready.

I leave with the bag and sip my iced tea as I walk home. When I reach the door, I immediately smell something familiar. It's the same perfume I noticed when I first met Damien. My heart skips. Someone is here. I hear a faint whispering.

I wish I had a gun or some weapon. My hands feel cold, but I force myself to move toward the bedroom. The door is slightly cracked. I reach out slowly, and my hand trembles as I touch it.

I push the door open just enough to peek inside.

Lydia is sitting beside Ollie.

The treasure chest beside her is the one that holds his Bible. She's humming softly, which sounds like a lullaby. I'm sure it's one from his childhood.

She looks up and sees me at the door, smiling as she gestures for me to come in and take a seat. Her eyes fall on the bag in my hands.

"What did you get?" she asks.

"I got broccoli soup and a ham sandwich for Ollie," I say, setting the food down. "And a salad and iced tea for myself."

Lydia smiles. "I know you love my son."

Her words catch me off guard. We barely know each other, and I wasn't expecting such a direct, emotional moment. But she continues, her tone warm.

"I know you two will be happy together."

Ollie begins to stir. He opens his eyes and sees his mom sitting beside him. She reaches for his hand and gently begins to speak.

"After you were shot, Harvey ran off. He went back to the cattle ranch near Rocky Creek. The man you were arguing with—the one about the missing cattle—he came back and tried to burn down the orphanage."

Ollie's eyes widen slightly.

"They started a fire on the front porch and in the living room," she says.

"But it burned itself out. There was some damage, but nothing too serious. If Vicki wants to return with the children, it's repairable."

I nod. "I'll talk to her when I see her at the Rebel settlement. We'll see what she wants to do."

Lydia smiles again. "Good. I think she'll appreciate hearing it from you."

Ollie seems comforted by her presence. Lydia then turns to me.

"I want to come with you when you go back to the Rebel settlement."

I hesitate, unsure if that's the best idea, but I keep it to myself.

"I can go get you something to eat," I offer. "If you want to stay with Ollie for a bit."

She looks surprised. "You're thoughtful. Thank you."

"What would you like? I mean, Lydia, I'll put my salad in the fridge while I go."

She shrugs. "I'm not too picky. Whatever Ollie's having is fine. Maybe some iced tea, too."

I nod and head out again, picking up another iced tea for her—one for me too, since I'm still thirsty.

When I return, I hand her the food, and the three of us sit and eat together. It feels calm, almost peaceful, after everything that's happened.

"I'll stay here for a few days," I tell her. "At least until Ollie's strong enough to go back to the settlement. I'm sure everyone is alright, and if I'm gone for a week, it won't make much difference. But I want them to know Ollie is okay."

As I reach for my salad, Lydia notices the ring on my left hand. She glances at Ollie.

"We're engaged," Ollie says, smiling softly.

Lydia seems pleasantly surprised. She smiles and says, "Congratulations."

I offer her the inflatable bed, but she declines. "The couch is fine," she says.

I get her set up in the living room, with a bit of help from Octavius and Ava. Honestly, I feel more at ease with Lydia here. She can keep an eye on Ollie if I need to step out—especially if the Others show up.

For dinner, I order pizza again, mostly out of habit. I didn't really think it through.

Ollie is staying awake longer now, even sitting up a little. I don't think it will be much longer before we can return to check on the group.

Later that night, Lydia falls asleep on the couch. I lie down on the inflatable bed, while Octavius and Ava sit beside a holographic campfire they've projected. Oscar keeps trying to swat at the flickering flames as they fade in and out of view.

I feel a wave of relief that Ollie is okay. I try not to think about the time continuum. At this point, I've caused so many disruptions—what's one more? Still, tomorrow morning, if Ollie is up for it, we'll head back to the Rebel settlement.

As I drift off, I watch Ava and Octavius quietly exploring the room. Oscar curls up beside me, and I finally fall asleep.

In the morning, I return to the café and order strawberry pancakes with whipped cream. I grab iced teas for everyone. The smell of the pancakes makes my stomach growl on the way home.

Ollie tries the pancakes and nods. "These are really good."

He's sitting at the dining room table with us now, and Lydia beams with joy seeing how well he's recovering.

I think about leaving Ava, Oscar, and Octavius here, but I don't know what we might run into. I decide to take them—just one last time.

I gather everyone and activate the Ether device.

We pass through the portal and land on the ground in the same field. The morning is quiet and sunny. I stand up and glance around. It's peaceful —too peaceful.

Ollie and I start walking to the right, heading toward the settlement. Lydia follows closely behind. I feel it again—that sense that we're being watched.

As we walk, I spot the Rebel settlement up ahead. A little wave of excitement rises in me. I hope it won't take long to find the group—we need to get Ollie back home soon so he can rest more.

We step into the settlement, but no one acknowledges us. It feels strange. Last time, we drew a lot of attention. I know we left the Rebels in an awkward position, and I'm not sure how that played out after we disappeared.

We head toward the apartment where we last stayed. As we get closer, a woman approaches us from behind.

"You'll want to go to the tribe's settlement," she says. "Everyone's there."

I recognize her—the same woman who brought us the welcome baskets of food last time. There's something different in her face now, a guarded expression.

"Is everyone okay?" I ask.

She hesitates. "They're alright. But not everyone will be happy to see you back… not with the uncertainty about what you plan to do with the time continuum."

I nod slowly. "I understand. I know the tribe's anxious about the possibility of going back to 1880."

We continue toward the tribe's settlement. As we walk, people avoid us —no eye contact, no greetings. Still, it's better than being surrounded or attacked. I can see Ollie is getting tired, and if we don't find anyone soon, we'll head back. This may have been the wrong time to visit.

I decide I'll leave a message with one of the tribe members to let our group know Ollie is alright.

Then, from behind us, I hear someone yell my name. I turn around as Vicki runs up, beaming with excitement.

She throws her arms around me. "You're back!"

I hug her tightly. "How is everyone?"

"It's going fine," she says. Then she notices Ollie and gasps. "You're okay!"

"He's doing much better," I say. "We just came to check in."

Vicki's eyes light up. "The group is talking about building a church here. And my first choice for pastor… is Ollie."

Lydia glances at me, and I know exactly why. I meet her look, then turn to Vicki, who is still smiling.

"There was only minimal damage to the orphanage," I tell her. "If you want to return, it's repairable."

Vicki pauses, caught off guard. Her smile falters for a moment.

"You didn't expect that," I say softly.

"No," she admits. "I guess part of me thought it was gone for good."

She doesn't say she's disappointed, but I can feel it in the silence that follows.

Raquel sees us and hurries over, wrapping me in a hug. A moment later, Anslow approaches with a big smile. One by one, the rest of the group comes forward, saying hello and asking about Ollie. There's genuine happiness on their faces, and I can tell—they all want to stay here.

I didn't expect this. I thought they would be eager to return to their old lives, back before any of this started. But I was wrong.

Then I hear another voice behind me. One I know all too well.

I turn around.

It's Matilda. She's standing there with Wendell and Ms. Collins. I glance around but don't see Damien.

Matilda looks more aggressive than usual as she starts walking toward us. Ollie steps forward, and she hesitates, stopping where she is. A second later, another voice cuts through the air. Just hearing it puts me on edge.

Red Fang.

The tribe is gathering, surrounding us, but I'm not afraid. I know God is with us. I know He will protect us.

Red Fang stands close to Matilda, and I can't help but wonder—have they joined forces? Or is this just a coincidence?

Louis and Anslow join our side, having noticed the growing commotion.

Red Fang fixes his gaze on me. "Give me the Ether device," he says.

"No," I reply calmly.

"I was hoping you'd say that," he answers.

Suddenly, the crowd falls silent.

Damien appears.

He walks forward slowly, dressed in cowboy gear, a long coat swaying behind him. In each hand, he holds an Ether device. Ava steps up in front of me, and Matilda moves forward, emboldened.

I can feel Red Fang watching me closely, trying to figure out where my devices are. I reach into my purse—I have two.

I look at Ollie and Lydia. "Should we leave?"

Lydia nods. "It's a good idea."

I pull out one device and check the coordinates. Good—it's set for the orphanage.

Just as I prepare to activate it, a boomerang comes flying from nowhere and knocks the Ether device out of my hand. I gasp and drop it.

The tribe cheers, and Red Fang comes closer, ready to grab it. But Matilda, unaware of her surroundings, steps in front of his horse. The animal swerves, and in the confusion, its hoof lands directly on the device.

The cheering stops.

I rush forward and scoop it up. It's cracked but intact.

Red Fang stands frozen, clearly realizing the mistake.

And now, everything shifts.

The device is still intact, but the coordinate screen is cracked. The numbers flashing on it don't look right. I'm not even sure if it still works—or where it would take someone if I used it now.

I glance up. Matilda is getting closer. I tighten my grip on the device, ready for her to try and snatch it.

Matilda locks eyes with Ava and laughs. "Look at you now," she sneers. "You don't have anything. No frying pan to swing at me, no hot air balloon to float away in. Nothing."

I glance at Ava. "This one's for you."

I activate the Ether device.

Matilda starts talking fast. "What are you doing? You can't use that—it's damaged. That's not fair."

The device begins to pulse. I can already smell the stale air filling the space around us. I aim the portal beam directly at Matilda, Wendell, and Ms. Collins. Then I turn slightly and look back at Ava.

"Want to do the honors?" I ask.

She hops up onto my shoulder, and I raise the device so she can reach it. Without hesitation, Ava taps the final button to activate the portal.

Matilda steps back, trying to distance herself from Wendell and Ms. Collins, thinking she can escape the beam. I quickly engage the EBAM function, expanding the beam in the last second to cover all three of them.

The Ether device activates with a sharp pulse. A swirling portal opens, and Matilda screams, shielding her face as she's pulled in. Wendell and Ms. Collins vanish with her.

The portal closes.

I turn toward the tribe.

"I have one more device," I say loudly. "So, unless you want to be sent back to 1855 right now, back up."

There's a murmur of surprise and a few uneasy shuffles. Then June steps forward.

"You wouldn't do that," she says calmly.

I meet her eyes. "If you don't move back with the rest of the tribe—I will."

THE TRIBE BEGINS to argue among themselves, each person trying to justify their position. I notice Damien standing nearby, silently observing with both Ether devices still in his hands. The debate goes in circles, rising with emotion but going nowhere.

Frustration boils over in me. Without another word, I toss both of my Ether devices onto the ground in front of everyone. Gasps ripple through the group.

All eyes shift to Damien.

"If you want peace," I say, looking straight at him, "then add yours to the pile."

He looks at Ollie, then Lydia. There's a long pause. And then he steps forward and places his devices on top of the others.

The crowd murmurs in disbelief.

I turn back to them. "If God doesn't want these devices to exist, then He'll destroy them."

There's a flicker of amusement on some of their faces. But then, out of the clear blue sky, a bolt of lightning strikes the pile. A blinding flash. In seconds, the Ether devices catch fire.

Red Fang rushes forward, trying to stomp out the flames. "No!" he yells.

But it's too late.

He looks up at me, stunned. "I guess your God wants us to stay in the future after all."

I nod slowly. "All of us. There's no way back now. Time travel is finished. The continuum is closed."

Vicki steps forward. "So… what will you do now?"

"I probably have it the easiest," I say, glancing at Louis. "We're from 2280. We still have homes. Small ones, sure, but something to return to."

Raquel speaks up. "Or maybe... You could stay here with us. We could build something new. Maybe start our own settlement, or join the tribe—or even the Rebels."

I look out at the crowd. My eyes meet Damien's, then sweep over the group.

"This is a chance," I say. "A real chance for peace. Between the dome cities, the Rebels, and the Others. We don't have to repeat the same old conflicts."

For a moment, no one speaks. The silence stretches, but it's thoughtful. People are listening.

Then June approaches me. Her eyes are warm, steady.

"My name," she says softly, "is Nizhoni."

I smile. "That's a beautiful name."

She returns the smile and turns toward Raquel, who reaches out and takes her hand.

I feel a light tug at the hem of my dress. I glance down and see Ava standing there, holding a bouquet of wildflowers.

She grins up at me, and in that moment, I realize—everyone here has caught onto something.

They want Ollie and me to get married. Right here. Right now.

Anslow steps forward, holding a Bible in both hands. He gives me a knowing smile and clears his throat.

He's ready to officiate.

An improvised wedding begins, and we say our vows, surrounded by our friends and the open sky. When it's time, we kiss, and I toss the bouquet into the air. Raquel catches it, laughing as everyone cheers.

"We'll still have a traditional wedding," Ollie says, looking at me, "once we build the church."

Everyone agrees that the spot where we just got married should become the church's future location.

As the celebration winds down, people begin to ask what we'll do next— whether we'll build a settlement here. Ollie and I decide that, for now, we'll return to the dome city until things are more stable.

The Rebels agree to let Raquel and Vicki stay in the apartment with the three orphans. Philip runs over to hug Vicki, and she puts her arm around him as they begin walking back to the Rebel settlement together.

Louis has his place, and Anslow is welcome to stay with him until he's ready to build his own cabin.

Lydia comes over and asks, "Do you think Damien and I could have a cabin built near where you and Ollie will live?"

"Of course," I say. "You're stuck here with us now, too."

As she turns, something catches my eye—a slim, black object in her back pocket. It looks like a TV remote. Or maybe… an Ether device.

That would explain what happened to the fifth one.

Ollie and I make our way back to the dome city for the night. Once we're home, he heads into his bedroom to lie down and rest. I hear the rustle of pages as he flips through the Bible he retrieved from the treasure chest bookcase.

Then he pauses. A small, folded piece of paper slips out and lands in his lap.

He picks it up and opens it.

"It's a deed," he says quietly. "To Red Mountain. My grandparents gave it to me."

He looks stunned.

"I don't know how I'll ever get back there to see them," he says, still staring at the paper.

I smile. "I think Lydia's already thought of that."

He looks at me. "What do you mean?"

"You'll know soon enough," I say, still smiling.

www.ingramcontent.com/pod-product-compliance
Lightning Source LLC
Chambersburg PA
CBHW072356030726
47505CB00014B/1858